A Kerry Marriage

By BIRDYE L. HARTLAND

Part 1 of the Shamrock Romances

Edited by Eva Valentine

A KERRY MARRIAGE
Originally published in 1900 by Thrilling Stories Committee and Birdye Latham Hartland
Copyright © 2020 by Eva Valentine

The information in this book is true and complete to the best of our knowledge at proof time. Although the author has made every effort to ensure that the information in the book was correct at press time, the author does not assume and hereby disclaims any liability to any part for any loss, damage, or disruption caused by errors or omissions, whether such errors or omissions result from scheming landlords, scandalized vicars, hysterical heiresses, morbid charladies, rascally youths, murderous magistrates, crazed cats, plague!!!, or any other cause.
P.S. Wear a mask! Wash your hands! <3

Ordering information: For more details, contact the publisher at victorianworkhousepress@gmail.com
Cover design by Black Widow Covers

ISBN: 978-1-953196-34-7

First Edition: November 2020

10 9 8 7 6 5 4 3 2 1 blast off!

Find all of the Shamrock Romance series at
https://victorianworkhouse.tumblr.com/

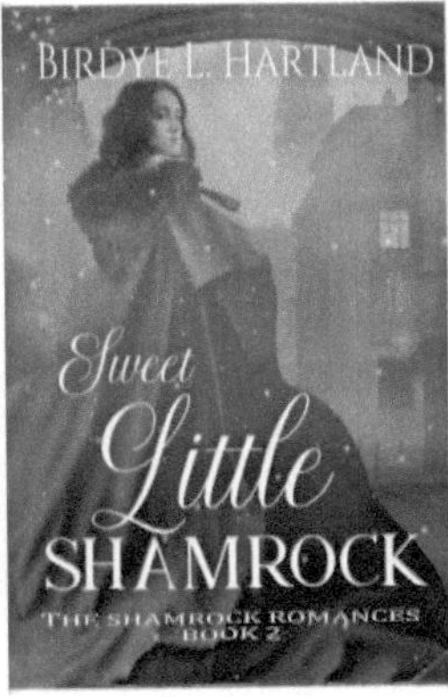

Grab the entire series today!
Book 1: A Kerry Marriage
Book 2: Sweet Little Shamrock
Book 3: Whom the Queen Honors

Heat level: No heat, sweet and clean

This is the Shamrock Romances series -- the first series
being released by Victorian Workhouse Press. We are a
tiny press dedicated to bringing back the old Victorian
penny novels and polishing them until they're sparkling
bright for today's readers.
Some people enjoy refurbishing old furniture; we love
refurbishing old books.

Table of Contents

Editor's Note

Sweet Little Shamrock, as well as all the other books in this series, was originally published in 1900 as a penny novel. This was a type of serialized novel that was published weekly in a cheap paper that cost, of course, only a penny. These serialized novels came to be called penny dreadfuls because, in some of them, the quality of the writing was just … dreadful. But some of these little stories were pretty good – and the readers at the time loved them.

I am a sucker for old books. When I was in high school, I read Victorian novels by the truckload. I got started on an old copy of *St. Elmo* that my grandpa had picked up at an auction, and read some of my books that my great-grandma had (I still have her old copy of *The Masquerader* by Katherine Cecil Thurston), and picked up many more via interlibrary loan. It's a love that still continues today.

I've been writing books for a long time, but I also love finding old books and editing them to bring them to a new audience. That's what I'm doing with these old penny novels. I'm transcribing them and editing them to bring them to the readers once more. These old stories are in the public domain, no longer under copyright, so anybody can do what they like with these old stories.

On one hand, it would be a lot easier to simply throw these little books out into the world, the way a lot of internet marketers are doing with books in the public domain. There are half a million (this is a very rough estimate) copies of *Pride and Prejudice* or *Anne of Green Gables* showing up on Amazon *every single day*.

A lot of internet marketers, looking for passive income, will grab a copy of some public domain book off Gutenberg, convert it into an ebook, and start selling it on Amazon.

I'm publishing these little books because I love those old Victorian books, and bringing these old books back to life is something of a fun craft project for me. I see stuff in the text that needs to be fixed, and I start fixing it, and the next thing I know, hours have passed and I'm sharpening the character motivation in Chapter IX. I spend hours cleaning up the text, which is a mess. Then I search for illustrations, format the book, proofread the pages, and get a pretty cover for it.

Pretty soon I have a tidy little book with a good story in it, ready to go, and I get a hiccup of pride. Look at that! I've rescued another little gem from the ash heap of history! It's a good feeling.

Some people enjoy restoring old furniture. I love restoring old books.

General Notes on Editing

Fond she was of the inverted style of sentence, so common in Victorian writing. "Well she knew no sympathy had he for all her misery" is one extreme example of this style of recursive writing which pervaded this story. Well would it be wise for me to add that this style was not a grave fault in those days.

Things have changed! These days, authors and readers prize simple sentences that cut quickly to the heart of the matter, instead of these sweet convolutions. The Victorian style called for a gentler, more flowery style of writing, which lend a grand, sonorous sound to the words, and make every moment seem epic.

Victorian readers also loved what today's writers would sneeringly call *sentimentality* – the teary-eyed, beautiful heroine struggling against a cruel world that did not understand her secret heart, that maligned her even as she strove to stay pure-hearted, raising her eyes to God, who alone heard her secret prayers.

While editing this book, I straightened some sentences that needed it. Our dear author (or perhaps her editor) apparently had a comma gun that they'd shoot at random into the text, because I must have excised half a million commas out of this book. British Victorian style also uses semicolons heavily; I removed them and tidied up the sentences if they weren't necessary.

I also added a great deal of text to heighten the tension, or to continue plot elements that the author dropped, or to add some details or a few lines to better explain the characters' motivations. I also added period details, reading old newspaper articles to understand the role that Ireland played in the South Boer War (though I have Opinions about the lousy role that the English played in colonizing South Africa).

I also added in a little bit about the attack that Charlie wrote about in one of his letters, because when I was reading the original text, I was so aghast at this boneheaded move by the British generals, to fling thousands of their troops into the cannon's mouth in this way, that I had to ascertain that it was true.

Seeking Information About Birdye L. Hartland!

I have been trying to find out anything about Birdye Latham Hartland, the woman who originally wrote these stories, but to no avail. I've searched the British Library, Google Books, Ancestry, FamilySearch, Google, Newspapers.com, and other sites, using different variants of Birdye's name and switching up searches. I thought that, because she had these stories published, that I would at least pull up a few hits. To my complete surprise, there has been nothing.

Now, I've done genealogical research and historical research with some hard-to-track women, and generally I've been able to find at least a few nuggets of information about them through one of these methods. I'm a little dismayed that I have not had any luck.

What's more surprising, to me, is that when you have a name with a unique spelling, such as Birdye, it's more likely to come up on genealogical sites. Not in this case!

I will keep searching for Birdye, even after I publish these books. Birdye deserves to have some credit for her work all these years later.

If any of you readers have any information about poor Birdye, do please send it along to me at <u>victorianworkhousepress@gmail.com</u>. No bit of information is too small, I promise. You'd be surprised how a seemingly inconsequential piece of information can turn into a full-blown lead in genealogy! I'll do the follow-up research and pop it directly into these books.

Anyway, I hope you enjoy this book. I plan to release these serials monthly, so follow me on Twitter at @VictorianReader and on <u>Tumblr</u>!

Be sure to buy these books, and tell your friends to buy them too, because at this time I am locked in a freezing garret in some Victorian slum by an evil taskmaster and I'm not allowed to come out until I've published about 56 of these books. Send bread!

All best wishes,
Eva Valentine, editor
Victorian Workhouse Press

FIRST EDITION.
No. 270—Thrilling Life Stories for the Masses—One Penny.
A KERRY MARRIAGE.
By Birdye L. Hartland
THRILLING STORIES' COMMITTEE, MANCHESTER.
Gordon & Gotch (London), Agents for Perth, Western Australia, Melbourne, Sydney and Cape Town

A KERRY MARRIAGE.

By Birdye Latham Hartland

Authoress of "A Struggling Family." "Lady Vernon's Heiress," "To Her Promise True," etc., etc.

CHAPTER I

THE O'DONOUGH was known far and wide throughout the whole countryside; everyone in Kerry had heard of him. Like a prince, he reigned among the people of the small, obscure, and most primitive village of Claisín.

"One of the rale owld stock," they called him, for the O'Donoughs had been great people in olden times; and though the property belonging to the family had gradually, but surely, diminished long before our story opens. The old homestead had fallen into decay, the long rent-rolls had dwindled down to a mere pittance. Still, it was evident that the glory had not departed from the ancient house of O'Donough, for all the county loved and respected the owner as a model landlord, true and kind to all, rich and poor alike.

The prefix of "The" had been used in the O'Donough family for centuries, in connection with the head of the house, instead of the more general term of "Mister."

The old, ancestorial residence for generations past, was a quaintly picturesque home nestled amid over-grown trees in a wild, romantic valley of West Kerry. It was just the place where one might surely expect to hear weird tales of rambling ghosts at nightfall, or the more fanciful legends of mysterious fairies, both of which are so interwoven about the simple and superstitious minds of the Irish peasantry, always on the alert for the supernatural.

Dewla O'Donough and her father lived here, in their secluded home, far removed from any neighbors, except, indeed, the poor tenants who lived upon the estate.

It was a peculiar life for a young girl to lead in books – girls dwell thus – but how seldom in real, actual life? Yet, strange to say, Dewla was never lonely – never felt time hang heavily upon her hands. On the contrary! The days passed all too quickly in her busy, young, healthful life. Left motherless at an early age, and being an only child, she grew up conscious of the grave responsibilities of her position, while even still a mere slip of a girl.

A cousin, somewhat older than herself, lived with them long as she could remember, her father having fetched the orphaned lad to share the hospitalities of their home, while she was still a baby.

Charlie Cooke and Dewla had therefore grown up together as brother and sister. She could remember shedding hot tears when the last days of the long summer holidays always came round, and he must return to college, leaving her behind to wander about through the old, deserted demesne alone.

She could not keep him always, she knew, for he had come of a long line of warriors, brave men in battle, who had laid down their lives for their country's sake. The army now must claim him, as it had done his father and forefathers before him.

The passing years that glided by, bringing so little change to Dewla in her far-off valley, brought many changes to her cousin, who was now a lieutenant in one of Her Majesty's regiments, stationed at Aldershot. His letters home, coming so regularly, were a source of great delight to Dewla and her father – to her, in particular, for it proved the only glimpse she got of the great unknown world, beyond the grey hilltops that bounded her life and home.

Summer passed into autumn. The green, fresh tints of the foliage had fled, giving place to the glorious hues of reddish-brown and gold. Each returning season was beautiful in Dewla's eyes. She loved the strange wildness of her country home, and welcomed the ever-varying phases of the year's circuit.

October was on the wane when a letter came from her cousin, bringing the news that he was ordered to South Africa, but would run home first, for a few days, to say good-bye.

War had just been declared with the Transvaal. Charlie came home, brimming over with excitement at the idea of being sent on active service.

"We expect to be back again in no time!" he cried gaily. "It won't take us long to lick the Boers."

"Oh, Charlie!"

"You needn't look so grave, uncle, for we mean to eat our Christmas dinner at Pretoria!"

"I cannot bear to think of war," Dewla said, shivering a little. "It *must* surely bring much suffering and death. Why cannot people live in peace?"

Charlie shook his head with the air of a general. "England can't knock under to the Boers," he replied hotly. "Oh! I shall have fine tales to tell when I return."

"May God grant that you return in safety!" said the O'Donough very gravely. "Ah, my boy, you know not what battle means. It is an awful sight – an awful sight. It changes you in ways that stay with you all your life."

Charlie glanced uneasily from his uncle to Dewla. How changed the old man looked during his months of Charlie's absence. Dewla had noted it with growing concern. When he walked now, his step was feeble, and his whole gait shaky.

"Are you quite well, uncle?" he enquired, noticing the thin transparency of the hand resting upon the old-fashioned, gold-headed cane which he always used.

"I don't feel quite myself, somehow," responded the O'Donough slowly, running his fingers through the white locks which curled upon his noble brow. "I get tired so easily! But come, we won't talk about it. When do you start, nephew?"

"On the first. All our fellows are impatient to be off."

The O'Donough sighed heavily, and turned his head away.

Later in the day, Charlie drew his cousin aside. "Dewie," he said gently, putting his arm about her in his old, brotherly fashion. "I feel anxious about uncle; he looks so unlike himself. Have you not noticed the change in him?"

"Yes!" she answered. "I am sure he is ill. Last week, I insisted on having the doctor visit us to see him, but he doesn't seem quite to know what is wrong."

Her cousin's face was clouded. "I am doubly sorry to leave you thus, Dewie. It may be a long, long time before we meet again, if ever," he added, more gravely.

The girl looked up into his face, a startled expression in her deep brown eyes. "Oh, Charlie!" she whispered. "I have no one else but you to whom I may turn in any trouble. You have always been as a dear brother to me. What am I to do when you are really gone?"

"Pray for us both, Dewie! Ask God to bring me back again in safety, and may He watch between me and thee while we are absent one from the other."

Dewla bowed her head reverently, for were not the words of his request a prayer?

The sun was setting behind the distant hills, the horizon was all aglow with golden splendor, and the evening breeze touched the whispering leaves.

In silence the young man stood, gazing long and earnestly at his companion's face. How fair she had grown, with a beauty, sweet and bewildering, all her own. He'd never seen a young woman who was half so beautiful as she; yet how unconscious she appeared, thinking nothing of her looks, as if she were still the little child with whom he used to play in the old, happy days.

As his eyes lingered upon her half-averted face, a conviction came upon him that, ere they should meet again, a change, great and momentous, would have taken place. Dewla would be the child Dewie no longer, and another would have the right to protect and love her. So real was the feeling, that he spoke his thoughts aloud.

"Dewie," he began impulsively, "I am persuaded that, when next we stand together, side by side, you will be to me as another person; even your name will have altered."

She started back as the meaning of his words dawned upon her. Then her merry laugh rang through the wood; it was too foolish for a moment's consideration.

"Cousin mine!" she cried, lifting her smiling face, "when you return, if it be in ten, or twenty years' time, you will find me here still, almost as you left me. There is none for me to wed were I ever so inclined – which I am not! Tell me, who, but yourself, have I known all these years?"

Then young Cooke shook his head. "Your argument sounds true enough," he returned, "and yet I feel confident my prediction will come true. Mark my words, Dewie, and remember what I say!"

"It sounds quite prophetic, Charlie," she retorted, laughing again, more gaily than before. "Pray be explicit, and tell me the name of my knight-errant?"

But he only shook his curly head. "Well, we shall see. Only don't forget to let me know in time, so that I may send you back a wedding gift! What would you fancy? Just give me a hint, please, and then I shan't have to cudgel my poor brains unnecessarily."

At this moment, a step sounded on the path, and her father's voice enquired what subject they were discussing so merrily?

Dewla turned her fair face towards him, all smiles and dimples. "Charlie asserts that I'll be married soon!" she cried gaily, "and I am choosing my wedding present!"

The old man started. Evidently, such an answer as this was unexpected. Hastily he glanced from one to the other as though he would read their thoughts, but the young man met his searching gaze with frank, clear eyes which defied deceitfulness in any form.

"My children, you should not joke on such a subject," he returned, almost severely. Then, with bent head, he passed on, continuing his slow walk towards the house, his mind full of a new idea.

His daughter's words awakened him fully to the fact that no longer was she a child, and may soon, alas! need another protector besides himself, for was he not daily losing strength and vigor?

This solemn conviction must be faced – it was useless trying to put it from him now. Covering his face with his trembling hands, he prayed God to guide him in the matter.

CHAPTER II

IT was the morning of Lieutenant Cooke's departure, but wanted yet some hours to the time when he must start.

"Let us take one round of the old lake, Dewie," Charlie said, with a touch of sadness in his voice. "You and I have spent so many happy hours there, in the days that are gone, that I'd like a look at it, just once before I go."

Very willingly his cousin complied with his request, and together they passed out through the old-fashioned hall, wandering down the long, pine-lined avenue, until they reached a wide expanse of water, just a mile in circumference, with arbutus trees growing at intervals along its sloping sides, dangling their strawberry-like fruits.

"How beautiful and calm it looks today," he said, a little absently; "hardly a ripple disturbs the tranquil surface! Would that your life and mine, Dewie, may prove as peaceful as this lake!"

In silence they stood, watching the sunbeams glance and glisten as they fell in golden flashes upon the water.

"You used to tell me a certain legend about our lough, Charlie, when I was a child; something about a great castle being buried somewhere at the bottom. Do repeat it again, for I have almost forgotten, and it was quite a nice little story if I remember rightly."

"It was old Jim Sullivan who told it me," returned her companion, "and he even went so far as to assert that his own father knew a man who recollected seeing the castle standing there, when he was a lad."

"Please, let me hear it once again," Dewla pleaded. "Try and fancy me the little kiddie whom you used to amuse by the hour, long ago, with your pretty fairy tales."

"That would be a little stretch of imagination," smiled the soldier, glancing down at her shapely head, with its coils of nut-brown hair. "Yet I can recollect you such a wee dot, in a white frock, and red sash, with a tangled mop of golden curls blowing on the wind. You ruled us both from the first – the O'Donough and me!"

Dewla laughed. "My reign is not over yet," she retorted, "so hasten, please, to obey my wishes, and let me hear the romantic tale of how the old castle got buried beneath the waters of the lake!"

Thus persuaded, Charlie complied, reciting the time-worn legend so commonly known in that part of the country. Dewla listened as eagerly as she had ever done in the old days of childhood.

For a long time they stood by the edge of the water's brink. So calm and quiet was the scene, that it soothed and rested their spirits.

"You'll not forget me, Dewie, when I'm gone?" Charlie asked at length, speaking his thoughts aloud. "'Tis nice to feel, when one's far away, that there's someone at home thinking of and praying about you. It helps to keep a fellow straight, you know, Dewie!"

"Every day I shall think about you, Charlie, and, in my humble petitions, your name shall never be missing."

She spoke so simply, just as she might have answered her own father, were it he.

It was evening, and Charlie Cooke had gone, leaving his pretty cousin very lonely and sad at heart, for farewells are always mournful, particularly in the time of war.

When would they meet again? That was the uppermost thought in both their minds, as their hands clasped for the last time.

The October day was drawing to a close. A bright fire burnt in the great, wide, open-mouthed grate, roaring halfway up the chimney. The long, paneled room presented a cheery aspect in the subdued light of a shaded lamp. The furniture was most quaintly old-fashioned – a trifle shabby now, perhaps, but that could not be helped.

Dewla sat on a low seat beside the glowing hearth, her dainty head with its wealth of auburn hair resting against the pillars of the carved oaken mantelpiece, black with age. A privileged white cat lay curled up contentedly upon her lap. Lost in thought, the girl gazed into the burning embers with grave, wistful eyes.

The O'Donough sat at some distance, busy with the contents of an open desk. A number of old letters lay scattered upon the polished table; these he had just been reading, slowly and carefully, one by one. His white head was bent, yet from time to time, he glanced furtively from beneath his shaggy eyebrows at the silent dreamer in the cozy chimney-nook.

Suddenly he lifted his worn face, and addressed her. "Daughter! I trust our young kinsman has said nothing foolish to thee, ere he left – nothing, I mean, of love, er such-like?"

The girl turned towards him, her eyes full of surprise.

"Most certainly not, father." she replied quickly. "Would you have us forget that we are cousins?"

"True, true, my child! I was unduly alarmed on your account. But did I not gather, from your conversation this morning, that that Charlie had mentioned the subject of marriage in some way?"

"Yes; but only in conjecturing that I should be Dewla O'Donough no longer when we meet again! Come, Papa. Cousins seldom marry in Ireland. Such an alliance is strictly forbidden by the Irish Church. You know that as well as I do."

The old man did not speak for a moment; then he took a letter, lying upon the desk, and peered into its contents. The writing was dull and faded, by long years of keeping.

"You have often heard me speak of my poor old schoolfellow John Smith, the best and truest of friends. He is dead now, many years; this is one of his letters." He tapped the creased and yellow paper gently with his forefinger.

"Yes, of course! Why, you've talked of him many a time, father."

"You remember, too, doubtless, that I am god-father to his only son, Hugh Jonathan, by proxy. Needless to say, I never saw the boy."

"But he writes to you occasionally, father; always at Christmas, and sometimes during the year – nice, kind letters, too."

"Yes!" returned her parent thoughtfully, as though weighing something in his own mind. "Yes! I think I'll write, and ask my godson here for a visit. I should like to see poor John's son before I die," he added hastily, by way of explanation.

Dewla started a little, for guests were most unusual ventures at Claisín; it was many years since any but Charlie had shared the hospitality of their old home.

"Dear, dear!" continued the O'Donough, as though talking to himself. "How proud poor John was of his first boy; surely it was the strongest proof of his great affection for myself, choosing me to be the child's god-father; it touched me deeply at the time. I remember. Yes! I should greatly like to see the lad, just for John's' sake— poor John. He and I were called 'David and Jonathan,' at school. Dear! dear! how long ago! Yet it seems but yesterday since we played together! Poor John!"

"You have an old photograph of your god-son's, father. I remember you showed it to me years ago. It was taken when he was quite a child; if I don't mistake, it is somewhere in that desk."

"Ah! true, true," and the old man began to fumble among the papers, stowed away neatly and carefully in the recesses of the worn and very antiquated writing case.

"Here it is," he exclaimed triumphantly, at length, after several unsuccessful attempts at finding it. "See! Poor John wrote the child's name and age on the back: 'My son and heir, Hugh Jonathan; aged two-years and a-half; your godson, called Hugh, after you.'"

And the O'Donough held the small carte-de-visite closer to the light, so that he might discern more clearly the infantine features of his little namesake.

Dewla rose from her low seat and drew near to her father's side, gazing at the photo in his hand with unusual interest.

"What a funny little kid," she said laughing; "and its clothes all seem too long! I wonder what Hugh Jonathan is like now?"

"If he is like his father, he is a good man," returned the O'Donough emphatically, "for I never met John Smith's equal."

"But what a commonplace name!" observed Dewla, meditating. "Why, John Smiths are as plentiful as blackberries, all over the country."

The old man frowned slightly at her words. "What's in a name?" he answered shortly.

Dewla had picked up the old-fashioned photograph, and was examining the child's face. As she looked upon it, a strange feeling stole over her, for she instinctively felt a presentiment that this same child, depicted here, would, in some way, influence her whole life. With a shiver, she laid it down again, the smile fading from her lips.

Without a word, she turned back once more to her old seat beside the chimney-corner. Clasping her knees with her small, brown hands, she gazed once again into the crackling fire, as though she fain would read the strange, unknown future written there.

Meanwhile, The O'Donough had taken up his pen, and written a letter of invitation to his unknown godson, begging of him for his father's sake to come immediately, as he feared his own days on earth were already numbered, and he had a great longing and desire to look upon his face before he passed away from this world to the next.

Folding the note with a deep sigh, the old man directed the envelope with shaking fingers, then rang the bell, and bade the servant have it sent in the mail bag that night.

"Dewla," he said, drawing his armchair closer to the fire, where she still sat, lost in thought; "it is my duty to tell you, poor child, that I feel my strength failing me strangely of late; no longer can I walk with ease. I would but prepare you, darling, for the worst if God should call me hence."

She started up, her eyes full of terror. "Oh! Father," she implored, "do not talk thus. Soon you will be better, and able to get about again, as of old. You are weak and nervous, dear – that is all."

But he shook his head. "I would not pain you, child," he answered softly, "only it will be lonely for you when I am gone. That is what troubles me most. I grieve to leave you alone in the world. If you were married, I should die more easily, for then I could feel that you had an earthly friend to comfort and shield your young life from harm and troubles."

Dewla had come to his side, and, kneeling down, clasped her arms about his neck with a little cry. "Do not talk so, Father; it distresses me so."

He patted her hand, but said no more about the shadow that was swiftly darkening over his soul.

CHAPTER III

MRS. JONATHAN SMITH, widow, lived at Trafalgar House in Hanley, a most smoky district of North Staffordshire. It was a modern dwelling, fitted with all the latest improvements of the age. Mrs. Jonathan Smith gloried, not a little, in the fact that hers was one of the most luxuriously-appointed houses in the whole district. All that money could do to beautify the place had been done, for the Smiths were immensely wealthy people. Here she reigned in state, living with her son and three daughters.

"The great lady," as people called her, had numberless acquaintances but very few real friends. She had ruled her husband in his lifetime, and now she essayed to rule his children. Even in her youth, she had had no pretensions to good looks. Now she was both very florid and stout.

"A most clever woman," her late husband used to say of her. Truly, her business-like capacities would put many a man to shame. At the time of his early marriage, people wondered much what the handsome, kind-hearted John Smith had seen in this woman, so utterly unlike himself in every way. Why he had chosen her above all other women as his own, always remained a mystery. No one could solve the problem.

It was afternoon at Trafalgar House. Mrs. Jonathan Smith and her daughters were seated in the highly decorated drawing-room. Something a little unusual had occurred, evidently, for the four were eagerly discussing some subject together.

"Fancy! Hugh deciding to fly off, literally to the ends of the earth – for surely Kerry is such – all just to please the caprice of an old man's foolish whim. I never heard of anything so absurd." Margaret Smith tossed back her head with a gesture of impatience.

"Who is this O'Donough, with the big "The" before his name?" enquired Etta, the youngest sister.

"An old school-chum of your father's," replied Mrs. Jonathan, shrugging her shoulders. "They had a kind of infatuation for each other – so much so, that your father chose him as godfather at Hugh's christening, though I had other, and better, plans in view. Sir Thomas Bigman would have stood for him with pleasure, I know, and would have been far more desirable than an impoverished Irish landlord, buried away in the wilds of Kerry! It was one of the few things which your late father did contrary to my wishes. I have ever since borne this O'Donough a sort of grudge, on that account." Here the great lady sat back in her easy chair with compressed lips.

"Imagine Hugh cancelling all engagements and starting off tonight on this wild goose chase. It seems most unnecessary." Mabel, the plainest-looking of the girls, tapped her foot impatiently upon the steel fender.

"It will be a bit awkward for us," announced Margaret. "We will have to make so many apologies! Tonight, for instance, at Mrs. Taunton's progressive whist party! Really, it is provoking, to say the very least!"

"Men are so very unreasonable," observed Etta. "A week or so later could make no difference to the old fogey in the kingdom of Kerry; and it would have been far more convenient to us."

"Hugh takes after his father in many things," replied Mrs. Jonathan slowly, as though the discovery was not altogether a pleasant one.

"The Sedley's dance is tomorrow night," broke in Margaret, "and Bella will be most awfully disappointed if Hugh is not present. Everybody, except himself, knows that she is very much smitten in that quarter."

Mrs. Jonathan smiled. She liked to have her son appreciated, especially by the acknowledged belle and heiress of the whole town. She, moreover, quite approved of Bella as a possible daughter-in-law and had even gone so far as to hint something of the kind to Mrs. Sedley.

"I fancy Bella is making a bit too sure of Hugh," remarked Mabel. "I don't believe he has ever given the subject of matrimony a serious thought. Most certainly, he is not one scrap in love with her."

Mrs. Jonathan frowned. She did not like to have her pet scheme set aside thus. Hugh would be sure to marry someday. Why should he not carry off this golden prize? That Bella liked him was most apparent; anyone with half an eye could see that. There and then she made up her mind to speak plainly on the matter with her son, as soon as he returned from his visit to Ireland. Indeed, she regretted now she had not done so before.

"Bella dresses so well," sighed Margaret. "She gets all her best gowns from Paris. She showed me her pale-green satin, specially designed for tomorrow night, and it is a perfect dream. I know she will be dreadfully cut-up when she finds Hugh is not there to admire it and her together."

Mrs. Jonathan smoothed down the ample folds of her silken skirt with her large, fat hand. "It is most unfortunate," she returned, "most unfortunate altogether, but we must only hope for his speedy return. Kerry is not exactly the place where one would wish to linger long – Hugh least of all."

"But this O'Donough has a daughter, has he not, mother?" asked Etta.

The great lady knit her brows, glancing reproachfully at her daughter. "A wild, half-educated hoyden! No fear of a son of mine so far forgetting himself, as to bestow a single thought upon such as that! No! When Hugh marries, his choice will fall upon a *lady*!" She emphasized the last word.

"But," persisted Etta, who loved an argument of any kind, "surely this O'Donough, whom father loved so well, is a gentleman. I am sure I remember father saying that he belonged to an old and most noble family."

"*Irish!*" spat Mrs. Jonathan, as if that one word embraced all that was low and vulgar. "I wish he were safely home again. I do not approve at all of this unnecessary journey. From the very first moment, I did my level best to oppose it – all to no purpose, evidently."

"Well, for your own peace of mind, mother," remarked Margaret, "let us hope Hugh will not be foolish enough to fall in love with this wild Irish girl, though I have heard it said that the maidens of the Emerald Isle are most beautiful."

Mrs. Jonathan again shrugged her ample shoulders. The drift of the conversation was growing most distasteful, and she hastened to turn the subject into another channel. "Mr. De Vere is invited for tonight's whist-party, is he not?" she demanded of her youngest daughter.

Etta's face burnt a deeper red, not at all caused by the warmth of the fire.

"Yes," she answered in rather ungracious tones.

Her mother's keen eyes regarded her fixedly for a few moments. "He is a long time hanging about you. I wish it would come to something."

"Not more than I do," retorted Etta angrily, starting to her feet, and shaking out the frills on her skirt.

"He seems to pay Maud Jefferies equal attention," observed Margaret in a bored voice, "and, indeed, other girls besides."

Mrs. Jonathan contracted her brows. "De Vere is handsome and rich," she said slowly, as though weighing the words carefully as she spoke them. "What more can a girl desire? No wonder he is much run after!"

Etta tossed her head impatiently. "I can't do any more than I'm doing," she returned in self-defense.

"Perhaps you are overdoing it," replied the old lady calmly. "I have known you to overdo things before."

Etta opened her mouth but, before she could speak, the door swung open and a young man strode in with quick, hasty tread.

"Good-bye, everybody!" he cried. "I'm off now. I have just enough time to catch the express." Stooping behind his mother's chair, he kissed her cheek.

"You are a silly to go," cried Hugh's sisters in a chorus.

"And fancy choosing to bury yourself in a remote corner of wild Kerry, instead of remaining comfortably here amongst civilized people!" rejoined Mrs. Jonathan, in tones of rebuke.

"Oh, well, it can't be helped," returned the young man cheerily. "I could not possibly refuse such a request from father's dearest friend; the poor governor often talked to me of him, and I know how much he loved the memory of their true and early friendship."

The matron rolled her eyes back in her head.

"Good-bye!" he called out again as he reached the door.

"Oh, good-bye!" retorted Mabel. "Don't fall in love with that wild Irish girl!"

Her brother paused in his rapid exit to laugh. "Not given that way," he shouted. Then the door closed, and he was gone.

Mrs. Jonathan sighed. If she loved anything in the world, beyond power and ambitious schemes, it was her handsome son, Hugh, who always brought sunshine into the house and considered her in everything, often putting his own wishes aside that he might please her.

"He is his father over again," she thought, "but only that, thank goodness! He inherits some of my practical common sense, and has none of John's romance and absurd sentiment."

She folded her plump fingers with an air of resignation somewhat foreign to her nature, for she was a woman who always got her own way in everything—one whom her husband used to say was born to command.

CHAPTER IV

HUGH SMITH was a fair specimen of a thorough Englishman: business-like and practical in all his habits, solidly unsentimental in ideas, and without the very least touch of anything even faintly approaching the romantic.

Steady, plodding, and shrewd, he bade fair to become, in time, a far richer and greater man than his father. Honorable and upright to the core, he was deservedly respected by all who knew him, either in private or public life. Such was the young man now journeying fast towards the out-of-the-way, straggling, and desperately poor village of Claisín.

Hugh Smith, as his unaccustomed eyes took in the almost bleak wildness of the uncultivated country scenery, shuddered rather to think how anyone could possibly prefer to exist in such a barren waste, so entirely cut off from the outer world, remote from all civilization. And yet it was here the friend, whom his father had loved so well, dwelt with his only child – contented, doubtless, to cling still to the ancestral home of his forefathers, with all the foolish pride of an impoverished Irishman of noble descent.

It was the last day of October. A glorious sun shone down upon the earth with almost summer heat. Hugh was seated somewhat uncomfortably on an outside jaunting-car – for such a conveyance was entirely new to him – and he found his "Jehu" driving the coach to be quite communicative.

"So, 'tis yourself is going to Claisín, sir! An' a fine, graver gentleman is the O'Donough himself, one of the rale auld stock, without a bit of a lie. Do I know him, sir? Sure an' bedad I does. Knows him all me life, sir, an' a better landlord never set foot in Kerry."

"Oh, good, good, good," said Hugh, checking his pocket watch.

"If there was more the likes of him, we wouldn't hear tell of murders, or boycotting, and the like. An' 'tis meself as says it! Why, there isn't no one as doesn't love him, for a good friend to the poor. And Miss Dewla, too! You be English, from your talking, sir, if I don't make too bold?"

"Yes, I'm English," answered Hugh, inwardly wondering if it was altogether safe to admit as much – for, after all, he was quite alone and unarmed in the very wilds of Kerry.

His driver threw back his head and laughed. "Well, sir, no blame to you for that! 'Tis a misfortune – ye can't help it! But I'm sorry for ye, sir, for all that."

"Sorry?" returned Hugh, surprised at the man's evident pity. "Why should you be sorry, pray?"

"'Cause, sir, the English isn't the same as us, at all. They haven't the same feeling! So they say, anyway; begging your pardon, sir. I don't mean no offence, seeing as you're English yourself."

Hugh laughed outright. This sort of argument was rather new to him, at any rate. The honest, good-humored expression of the driver's countenance showed him that the man meant, and believed, what he said.

Gazing enqu'ringly at the *stranger*.

"Is it much further to Claisín House?" Hugh asked as they passed through the little village, if such it might be called. Hugh eyed its irregular string of small cabins on either side, plainly proclaiming its terrible poverty and want of cleanliness to the world in general.

At the clatter of the horse's feet, a few women's heads appeared above the half-doors so general in the Irish cottages, gazing inquiringly at the stranger.

A few pigs were contentedly feeding in the gutter, while half-a-dozen children "huzzaed" him lustily in passing. They ran nimbly with their little bare feet after the car, trying to catch on to the back to have a ride, heedless of the driver who cracked his whip at them, crying loudly, "Get away witch ye, boys!" What merry, dirty faces they had, and eyes that twinkled with fun.

Something about them appealed strangely to the matter-of-fact Englishman. Whether it was their ragged, ill-fitting clothes, or sunny brows, he knew not; but he suddenly found himself fumbling in his pockets for some loose coins, which he flung to the mud-bespattered urchins.

With a ringing shriek of delight, they rushed towards the rolling money, tumbling over each other in their scrambling, all desirous of gaining a prize.

Hugh smiled as he turned round on his narrow seat to watch their fun. What a little thing, truly, had gladdened their hearts.

"You axed if 'twas far on to The O'Donough's, sir," said the driver. "Only 'bout three mile more Irish miles, I mean, sir. 'Twas a fine, old place wunst—'twas so, sir! There wasn't the like of it nowhere, for grandeur an' everything. But the bad times come along, an' them suffered terrible, more than other landlords, for they wouldn't press their tenants for pay, as did others. No! bless their honest souls, the Donoughs couldn't do the like

– 'tisn't in their breed. Oh, but they're a grand old family, the best in the land. Why, there's them as says the Queen of England isn't more noble-born than they."

"Flattering to Her Gracious Majesty," murmured Hugh Smith, much amused.

"The O'Donough himself is failing, of late," continued the talkative son of Erin, "and more's the pity, says I, for he'll leave none like him behind in these parts. Leastways, I'd like to see Miss Dewie 'settled' afore he goes; but there isn't none of her rank nowhere here."

"I suppose she looks too high," observed the stranger carelessly, his eyes wandering over the wide expanse of wild wasteland, disclosing nothing of beauty for him, for he saw not the grandeur of its untamed, natural magnificence. It was a dreary waste of bog to him, and nothing more.

"Too high!" echoed the driver, in tones of surprise. "There's none too high or mighty for the O'Donough's daughter. A prince of the throne might be proud to wed the likes of her – an' that's the truth, without a word of a lie!"

"Oh! By the way," cried Hugh, rousing himself into a show of interest, "I've heard queer tales about Irish country marriages. The match is made, not by the couples themselves, but their parents, or the parish priest – is not that so?"

"An' who'd know better?" retorted the other. "There isn't no foolish courtship afore marriage. I didn't lay eyes on me own Mary Ann till her 'accounts' were out, an' 'twas all fixed up for the next morning, atween her father and me own."

"Her accounts? What are they?" enquired the stranger, a puzzled expression on his face.

"Didn't the likes of ye ever hear tell of that?" asked the driver, evidently much surprised by his companion's great and appalling ignorance. "The accounts is the fortune, of course – how many pounds – how many cows or pigs! That's the way they settles it. When a man wants his daughter married, he just sends out her 'accounts' – Shrove is the great time; just before Lent, you knows – an' he hears of a 'likely' young man with a bit of a farm, whose parents wants a wife for him. So the old people, they meets in the back-room of a pub, generally, and there they come to terms, or knock it off altogether, if they can't agree as to the bit of money."

"Is this really true?" gasped Hugh. "It seems so very odd to me, especially among the Irish, who are proverbially so romantic, in character as a nation!"

"Of course, 'tis true, sir," retorted the other, a little offended by his companion's want of faith in his words.

"Why, we wouldn't tolerate such an arrangement in matter-of-fact England," returned Hugh. "It seems to me a most peculiar way of settling affairs. Are the people ever happy, may I ask, who are married in this strange manner?"

"Of course they is, yer honor! An' why not? But here we are at Claisín. That's the house: ye can see it atween the trees."

Through the old, dilapidated gateway they drove, and down the long, tree-lined avenue, until they stopped before a large grey pile of building, irregular in shape, and ivy-grown in parts the remains of what had once assuredly been a most princely mansion, now fallen into much decay and neglect.

Hugh Smith, accustomed to a more modern dwelling house, well-kept and trim, almost shuddered as he contemplated this house, which to him seemed a mere pile of ruins. His keen eyes took in everything at a glance – the cracked panes in the church-like windows of the upper story, the long-worn paint upon the woodwork, the neglected "sweep" in front, where grass grown in patches, and the ungraveled drive. The rare architecture in the quaintly planned edifice passed unnoticed; he saw only the somewhat loosened stones in parts, and other apparent signs of coming ruin.

"What a place to live in!" he said under his breath as he sprang down from the rickety seat of the antiquated outside car. "I wonder what the inside is like, and how I shall like my unknown host and his daughter, this haughty damsel, who considers all mankind beneath her gracious notice?"

Striding towards the front entrance with its curiously carved archway pillars, he rang the rusty-looking door bell, which pealed and echoed again and again through the whole building in ghostly fashion.

"Sounds as though the house is empty," he reflected uneasily, glancing at his luggage. "What a rum lot these Irish people seem to be."

But at this moment his meditations were abruptly cut short by the opening wide of the heavy, massive door, which creaked upon its hinges.

"Is The O'Donough at home?" he enquired of the rosy-faced, rustic maid.

But before she could reply, a light step sounded upon the polished floor. A girl, wearing a soft, white dress, advanced quickly, with extended hand.

"You are Mr. Smith?" she said simply with a lilting accent in her voice. "Father has been expecting you all the afternoon. He is not very well today, and is obliged to remain in his own room."

And Hugh Smith, looking down upon her uplifted face, thought he had never seen so fair a picture.

Across the wide hall, stripped now of much of its original beauty, she led him, and up the old-fashioned, winding stairs. An architect would have raved about the quaintness of the plan of the house, with its oak-paneled walls and rambling corridors; but this stranger saw only the worn carpeting beneath his feet.

Dewla did not speak again until she paused before a closed door at the end of the deserted-looking passage. Here she knocked gently.

"This is father's room," she said. "He will be glad to see you, I know." Then she turned swiftly away.

CHAPTER V

"BUT, sir, your daughter does not love me!" Hugh said in disbelief. "How can she? I have been here but two days, and even in that short time I have seen little of her, except when you are present. She is so shy and quiet, only answering me when I put a question directly to her!"

"And how would'st thou have the child?" cried the old man impatiently. "Surely not pert and forward, as the 'New Woman' of the present day?"

"Nay, sir. She is sweet and perfect in my eyes, like no other girl whom I have ever met; but plainly she shrinks from me, avoids my approaches in every way."

"Pooh!" retorted the O'Donough. "It is but maidenly coyness. She is shy with you, doubtless, for with the exception of her cousin now called to the front, she has known few men. I was glad, from the first, to see that you liked her; for I should desire nothing better than to see the son of my best and oldest friend united to my only child. I dreamed even of this before you came!"

"Does she your daughter know of that?" enquired Hugh quickly.

"No. It is not our custom, in these parts, to consult our daughters' wishes in such matters. The parents, surely, are older and wiser judges, and know what is best for their children. We follow the good and ancient examples given us in Holy Writ. What guidance could be better?"

Hugh was silent then.

The two men were seated in the large and, to the stranger, draughty drawing-room, used now specially in honor of the distinguished visitor's presence in the house. Here had been lavished a wealth of decorations in the old days, now sadly spoiled by time's rough hand and somewhat defaced by damp and long neglect. The daughter of the house seldom sat here. There were none of the many signs of a feminine element about the room, such as Hugh had noticed in the cozier sitting-room, where stood a work basket, paintboxes, and sundry other such things.

It might, perhaps, look better in summer, Hugh reflected; but now, with the almost-leafless, rain drenched November trees swaying to and fro outside the deep-seated windows, he found it dismal in the extreme.

True, a great fire burnt in the huge grate, but much of its warmth appeared to escape up the wide, old-fashioned chimney. Hugh shivered a little as the sound of the pattering rain grew louder upon the window glass.

"You say you care for my daughter, Hugh?" the old man asked, after a somewhat lengthy pause.

"Yes!" returned his guest. "I admire her in every way, more than anyone I have ever met before; but I do not say I actually love her. And I am perfectly certain that she does not, in the least, love me."

"Oh! That's nothing!" returned the O'Donough emphatically. "Love will grow in time! Shall I ring and summon Dewla, so that she may know of our arrangement?"

Hugh started. Unromantic as he was by nature, such a course fairly took his breath away.

"Not for the world, sir!" he cried. "I would not gain your daughter's consent in this way. If I am to win her affections, it must be in a different way altogether."

"As you will," answered the old man, a trifle coolly. "You shall do as you wish. However, my days are drawing to an end, and I fain would know my precious child was entrusted for life to your care, before I close my eyes in death. The time is short – shorter, perhaps, than I know of."

For some moments Hugh Smith sat, leaning his face upon his hand. He had never been thrust into so bewildering a situation in all his life before, and he hardly knew what course to pursue.

From the first, he had been much impressed by Dewla's beauty, and, during their two days' acquaintance, his regard had deepened considerably. The simple shyness of her manner when she spoke to him attracted him strangely, and her evident love and consideration for her father pleased him much, for she was ever trying to ease his pain, and add to his comforts.

With an impatient gesture, Hugh sprang suddenly to his feet and walked towards the deep-set window.

Outdoors, the rain had ceased, and the dying November sun struggled for mastery with the dull, grey clouds. Heavy raindrops still pattered from the overhanging trees, splashing upon the grass-grown gravel walk.

Lost in thought, the young man gazed out, with slightly contracted brows, upon the somewhat dismal scenery.

"Suppose, sir," Hugh began, suddenly wheeling round towards his host, "your daughter and I take a short walk together. The rain has stopped, and she tells me she is used to being outdoors in all weathers. We might get to know each other a little better. As it is, we are still almost strangers. "

"As you wish," returned the elder man gravely, "but bear in mind that, in these parts, so-called courtship is deemed unnecessary. A maid accepts the suitor provided for her by parental wisdom. Needless to say, no child of mine would, for a moment, gainsay my wishes! But, of course, you English people prefer your own unorthodox course. Speak to Dewla herself if that would please you best. Stay; I'll ring for her."

"Send your mistress to me," The O'Donough said a moment later to the domestic who appeared in answer to his bell.

In a singularly perturbed state of mind, Hugh Smith returned to the window as though he would seek consolation from the misty landscape beyond.

Presently Dewla herself entered, and, advancing towards her father, inquired of his pleasure.

"Our guest," her father said, glancing towards the tall figure by the casement, "desires that you would walk with him. The rain has passed off again. Hasten, my child, to put your bonnet on."

"But you, father – shall you not feel lonely, if we both leave you?"

"Nay! My daughter, do as you are bidden. Take your friend to see the lough. The walk is pretty, even at this unlovely time of year."

With a quick, enquiring look at Hugh, Dewla left the room without further remonstrance.

The young Englishman had never, perhaps, felt more awkward than now, as he and his fair guide sallied forth together.

"What a curious old place," he began, anxious to start some kind of conversation.

He spoke at a venture, but, evidently, he could have chosen no better theme, for instantly the girl's face brightened, and her eyes glowed.

"Oh, I love it!" she cried with all the warm enthusiasm of her race. "Every tree and stone is dear to me. I would not change my dear home, here, for a queen's palace."

Hugh looked down at her in some surprise. Why she adored this dilapidated estate on the road to ruin, was rather a mystery to his prosaic mind. But he dared not give vent to his thoughts.

Poor girl, he thought. Perhaps she has never been in a modern, comfortable, and wealthy homestead!

"But you should see it in summer, or even autumn," Dewla added. "Oh! It is so much more beautiful. I never tire of admiring all its many perfections."

"More beautiful," thought Hugh. "What is she thinking of?" He glanced about him on all sides in search of something that would justify her evident admiration.

Dewla noticed his silence, for she said impulsively, "Do you not love the country, Mr. Smith?"

"Well," he returned, a little doubtfully, "I can't say I should care to live in a place like this always." Whatever faults Hugh had, he was honest to the core.

She looked up with eyes full of real disappointment. "I am sorry," she said, in a low voice, "but then, I am foolishly fond of my home. It is a failing with most Irish people, I believe."

"The English are just as proud of their homes," laughed her companion, "every whit. An Englishman's home is his castle, you know."

"Then is your home more beautiful than mine?" she enquired in serious tones.

Hugh smiled at the mere comparison. "Trafalgar House is supposed to be one of the finest and best furnished abodes in our large district."

"But the grounds – what are they like?" she asked quickly.

"Grounds! Oh, we have really none! Just a flower garden, about which my mother is most particular, and a small croquet-lawn with a tennis-court – that is all."

"But have you nowhere to wander about at will, under trees, on mossy paths like these?"

"Oh, no! We English are not a sentimental race," laughed the young man, much amused.

Dewla was silent. She felt she could not quite understand him – he was so different from her cousin Charlie.

"Are you not lonely here, Miss O'Donough?" he enquired presently. "No near friends, or visitors, to enliven the dullness of your life?"

"My life, dull?" she cried. "Oh, you mistake. I am never tired of it – never!"

Hugh looked incredulous. "Why, my sisters would simply die if they lived here; it would be as bad as a nunnery, in their eyes."

"Will you tell me about your sisters? Do, please; I should so like it. I have never had sisters."

"I don't know what there is to tell," he returned, rather at a loss as to how to comply with her wishes.

"How do they spend their time each day, for instance?" she said.

"Oh, as girls usually do, I suppose – seeing after things in general, shopping, paying calls, and receiving visitors. Then, at night, there is always something going on – they do the carpet dances, whist-drives, concerts, and so forth in the winter. In summer, they play tennis, croquet, cycling, and golf."

"It sounds like a perfect whirl of activity," returned the country girl slowly. "And yet, though I have none of these, I am very happy and contented here."

By this time they had almost reached the picturesque lough, a full view of its wide expanse of water bursting suddenly upon their gaze.

"See!" cried Dewla, pointing. "There is our beautiful lake. I love to come and sit upon the low wall yonder, watching the tiny ripples on the water's silvery surface. Is it not pretty? But when the trees are quite green and fresh, you would see it at its best."

Decidedly unenthusiastic by nature, Hugh found it hard to rise to her pitch of admiration.

"Have you no boat?" he enquired, searching in vain for any sign of one, or even a boathouse.

"No, but my cousin, when he lived with us, made such a funny kind of raft, and he and I used to take trips across the lough on it. Oh, it was such fun! How we used to enjoy it. More than once we both fell in, and then we had to steal back to the house, so that father might not see us."

"But was it not wrong to deceive your parent?" enquired Hugh gravely.

Dewla looked up swiftly, and the hot color dyed her cheeks.

"You do not understand," she answered proudly. "It was simply not to distress him. Of course, he knew about our raft, and often came to watch us. We would not have used it against his knowledge or wishes."

Hugh watched her face in silence. What a curious mixture she seemed – one moment so sweet and gentle, the next, proudly resentful of the smallest rebuke.

"And you really do love this place?" he said, his eyes wandering around the wild, deserted landscape, with not a single habitation of any kind in view.

"Of course I do," she returned, with considerable warmth. "I should not be a true O'Donough if I loved not the home of my forefathers. But, even apart from that, this lough is full of romantic interest."

"Indeed! In what way, may I ask?"

Dewla hesitated, feeling instinctively that her companion would not sympathize with the pretty legend of the buried castle – not as she and Charlie did – and how the lovely maiden escaped marriage with one whom she did not love, but remained ever true to the brave knight who had won her heart.

"Well?" questioned Hugh again, seeing that she made no reply.

"They say a castle once stood where the waters now roll, but that it got covered in some mysterious way."

Hugh laughed. "Such unlikely tales are told about most lakes," he returned, not meaning in the least to hurt her feelings. "You Irish people would believe anything credulous to the last extent."

Dewla turned away her head and gazed in silence upon the lough she loved so well. How short a time ago it seemed since she and Charlie had stood together on this very spot. And now he was far away – how far, she knew not.

Tears started to her eyes as she thought of her dear cousin and companion of her childhood hours.

"You seem in a pensive mood, Miss O'Donough."

The words made her start a little. She had, for the moment, forgotten herself.

"Excuse me," she said hurriedly. "I was thinking of my soldier-cousin. His regiment has been ordered to South Africa."

"Yes, I think your father mentioned something of the kind. But had we not better return to the house? It is cold standing here, and the ground is quite wet still – that is, of course, if you can tear yourself away from this romantic spot?"

In obedience to his wishes, Dewla turned instantly away from the lake, with the grey shadows of evening gathering upon its clear, still surface.

Hugh found her quite reserved as they walked back to the house over the neglected pathways, though he tried to draw her into conversation on many points. At length, however, he mentioned her father. Then she was all attention.

"Do you think he seems worse since you came?" she asked, her lips quivering like a child's.

Hugh noticed her distress and tried to find words with which to comfort her. But she would not be put off thus.

"I know he is worse," she faltered, her eyes filling with tears. "I can see it plainly, though he tried so hard to hide the fact, and insists on coming downstairs as usual."

He knew it would be false consolation to say that her father was going to recover. In a voice unusually grave and gentle, he said, "Miss O'Donough, I have lost a father. I perfectly understand and sympathize with you, in this time of deep anxiety and trouble."

She bowed her head, touched by his words and manner. A faint color rose to her pale cheeks. At times, this handsome stranger chilled her beyond measure; but when he spoke thus, it seemed to thrill her whole being with joy.

"My father," continued Hugh in a husky voice, "was the one I loved best on earth; he was, indeed, everything to me. No one knows but myself how keenly I miss him, even now, though it is years since he died."

He said the last words in a whisper, as though the memory of that death was too sad and sacred even to touch upon.

"And my father loved him, too," answered Dewla softly. "He has always talked of him in terms of deepest affection. I can quite feel for you in your loss, but..." and her voice grew lower – "your loss was Heaven's gain. That is the one great comfort, surely, which steals the bitter sting from death's dark pain!"

Hugh Smith listened with a strange feeling of surprise and reverence. This shy, quiet, little Irish maiden was unlike anyone else whom he had ever met or known in all his life before. He was growing more interested each hour, as stray glimpses of her inner nature were occasionally revealed to him.

On over the sodden path they went in silence, where the fallen leaves, blown together in untidy heaps, were left to lie undisturbed, soaked by the recent heavy rains. They had almost reached the grey, rambling mansion.

Hugh could see the old man's face watching out for their return from one of the lower windows.

"Your father waits for us," he said.

Dewla, lifting her eyes, hastened forward.

"I have not made much progress, I fear," mused the stranger to himself as he followed.

CHAPTER VI

THAT evening, after making sure that her father had all that that he needed for the night, Dewla retired a little earlier than usual. She left the two men talking together in the small ante-chamber adjoining the O'Donough's room, where the firelight seemed to play at hide-and-seek among the quaint, old furniture – a trifle heavy-looking, perhaps, for modern taste.

The girl's heart was lighter than it had been for some time. Her father seemed so wonderfully bright and better that a ray of hope began to dawn on the darkness of her horizon. Ah! God was surely going to leave him with her a little longer. She could not do without him yet, for without him, she was so sadly alone in the cold, great world. With a thankful heart, she laid herself down, falling quickly into a deep, restful sleep.

She might have slept thus an hour or more when she was awakened suddenly by a gentle tap upon her door. Starting up affrighted, she found Hannah, the old servant who had been her nurse, standing outside upon the landing.

"Miss Dewla, honey-bawn, the master's had a turn. He didn't feel well soon after you left him. Mr. Smith wouldn't go to bed, he felt that anxious. Then, when he didn't get no better, we sent for the doctor, who is here now. The master wants you, honey. He asks for you constantly!"

Hardly waiting to hear the woman's last words, Dewla began hurriedly to dress. Her father ill, and wanting her! That lent swiftness to her fingers, trembling though they were.

In an incredibly short time, she entered the O'Donough's room. Hugh and the doctor stood aside to let her pass, but she seemed to notice neither. Her eyes were fixed upon the pallid face lying upon the white pillows, which nearly matched the extreme pallor of his face.

"Dewla, my daughter," he whispered, as she bent over him in voiceless anxiety. "I am going soon to rejoin your dear mother in the land where no parting is. Kiss me, my child, and tell me that you love me well."

"Oh, father, surely you know that I do!" she cried in a low, agonized voice. The old man beckoned Hugh to his side and whispered in his ear. Then, silently, Hugh drew the doctor from the room, leaving Dewla and her father alone.

"My child," murmured the sick man, "the hours of my life are numbered – nay, do not weep! Before I die, I desire most earnestly to see you wedded to my old friend's son in yonder room. Are you willing to gratify my last solemn request?"

The girl started back. Surely, nothing was further from her thoughts at this sad moment.

Her father saw the movement, and waited anxiously for her answer.

"I have never disobeyed your wishes," Dewla sobbed at length, "but this – this is different."

"It is my most sacred wish," he replied. "Do not disregard my dying request, will you, Dewla?"

Finding no answer ready, she hid her face in her hands.

"Hugh wishes it above all else. He will be good and loving to you, my child. I shall die happy, when I know that your future belongs to him. Speak the word, child! Our kind pastor is even now on his way hither, to administer to me the blessed sacrament of our church. May he perform a double office, in uniting you both, my dearly-beloved children, in holy matrimony?"

For some moments there was a death-like stillness in the dimly-lighted room.

Then, in a choking whisper, Dewla murmured, in a broken voice, "It shall be as you desire, father. I have never disobeyed you yet, and I shall not now!"

The old man drew her to his breast and kissed her tear-stained cheeks. His strength was ebbing fast away, and the effort cost him much.

"Summon Hugh!" he said faintly. "I would speak with him a while."

With faltering steps she obeyed, giving her father's message with averted face and downcast eyes. Hugh understood her evident distress. Taking her unwilling hand in his, he stooped down and whispered, "If it is not your wish, it shall not be."

The warm color swept across her face. For a moment she seemed to hesitate and waver.

Then, looking up into his face, she said like one speaking in a dream, "What my father asks, I dare not refuse."

Only half-satisfied, Hugh turned from her, returning to the sick man's side.

Surely it was a strange, strange wedding. The darkly-paneled room, dimly lighted, with the very presence of death brooding over it. The old man's face so eager, though his breath came short and fast.

Hugh, grave and reverent; Dewla, pale and trembling, scarce able to frame the words which bound her for life to the man who stood, erect and proud, at her side. Her beautiful hair, which, in her nervous haste, she had forgotten to bind, hung at will far below her waist. As she now bent her head, it fell in a bright shower, veiling her face from view.

Surely no service could be more solemn – the clear, earnest voice of the minister filling the room. Life was ending for the old man who was so soon to cross the borderland of the unseen world beyond; his feet were already touching the cold waters of Jordan. Life beginning for the two who now pledged their troth, taking each other "for better, for worse; for richer, for poorer; in sickness and in health, to love and to cherish, till death do us part."

With feverish anxiety the dying man seemed to listen, straining his dulled ear to catch each word.

Like one in a trance, Dewla stood, scarcely conscious of the all-importance of this sacred hour. There had been no time to think, no leisure in which to ponder and weigh the issues of the future.

Such hastily-arranged marriages were common enough with the people among whom she dwelled; from a child, such tales were familiar. But, even at this grave moment, it was of her father she thought most, and of pleasing and obeying him alone.

Now, as she turned her eyes upon her father, when the concluding words were spoken, she saw with horror the change upon his face – the ashy whiteness, the drawn expression.

With a stifled cry, she flew to his side.

"My darling! My little Dewie! God bless thee in this life and the next! May we all meet—" But he paused; the words died upon his blue, cold lips. With a last sigh, her father's head relaxed back into its pillow.

The doctor took her father's pulseless hand in his, and laid it gently upon the counterpane.

There had been no struggle. Like a child, wearied by play, he fell asleep; but that sleep was the long, unwaking sleep of death.

"It is all over," the doctor said, in a low undertone, but the orphaned girl caught the words, and knew, alas! their import.

Her slight form swayed, and she would have fallen, had not Hugh caught her in his strong arms. Tenderly he bore her from the room, his heart full of pity for the sorrow-stricken daughter, whose life henceforth would be intertwined with his own.

CHAPTER VII

"GIRLS!" cried Mrs. Jonathan Smith, in tones of horror, a letter fluttering in her hand. "Girls! Hugh is married!"

"Married!" echoed three shrill voices in a chorus.

The announcement was unmistakably unexpected, and, evidently, very unpleasant, too.

"Mother, what do you mean?" continued the eldest, for the others were silent again.

Mrs. Jonathan's florid face was almost purple. "I can hardly believe the evidence of my own eyes!" she went on, turning her distracted attention once more upon the hastily-scrawled letter. "Listen to what he says," she cried.

Claisín, Nov. 4, 1899

My Dear Mother,

I have two things of importance to communicate, viz., my own marriage with Dewla O'Donough, and her father's sad death, which occurred immediately after the ceremony. It was, in fact, on account of his approaching end, that our marriage was hastily arranged.

My poor little wife (how strange the words look) is overcome with grief. We will remain here until everything is finally arranged. But I will write again.

You are sure to love Dewla, not only because of her relationship, but for her own sweet self. Love to the girls.

In haste, your affectionate Son,

HUGH J. SMITH.

Mrs. Jonathan half-collapsed in a chair, fanning herself with the letter.

"Well!" cried Etta, "I've heard that Kerry marriages were funnily arranged, but, surely, this beats them all! Fancy! Hugh sensible Hugh being taken in and done for."

"I believe he was 'taken in,' and cruelly so!" returned Mrs. Jonathan with tightly-compressed lips. "All this needs to be carefully inquired into. To me, it is simply monstrous!"

"But it is too late now," observed practical Etta. "If, as Hugh says, he is married, what more can be done? The thing is all at an end. But won't this news be a shock to the Sedleys! I should not like to be the one to inform Bella. Really, I can't believe it yet!"

"I wonder what she's like?" conjectured Mabel.

"Countrified, of course, in the extreme – fat, red, and freckled!" cried Margaret. "Oh, dear! Shall we have to introduce this sister-in-law into our circle of acquaintances?"

"It is really dreadful," declared Mrs. Jonathan, who had never been so upset in all her life. "And the worst is, nothing can be done now, except to receive this Irish hoyden as one of the family."

Mabel put her hand over her heart and gasped in a very fake way.

"I never heard of anything more provoking," Mrs. Jonathan continued, shaking the letter until it rattled. "What food for gossips it will give! There will be no end of tales circulated at once." Tears of anger and disappointment stood in her light-blue eyes.

"He might have considered us a little," retorted Margaret sullenly, "for, of course, a low connection such as this will injure our prospects not a little. It is bound to do so!"

Mrs. Jonathan looked helplessly from one daughter to the other.

"I was much set against this Irish trip," she declared. "From the very first, something seemed to tell me that it foreboded nothing good. But Hugh was positive; and now you see what evil it has brought upon him, and us. A man of his position and prospects allying himself thus with a wild, uneducated Irish girl, about whom he knows nothing! It is enough to drive one crazy! He, too, who might, have wedded the best in the land." With this open display of her deep disapproval, she covered her eyes with her cambric handkerchief.

"But some Irish people are nice," responded Etta. "I like the few I have met. There is something honest and trustworthy about them; besides, they are acknowledged to be brilliantly witty."

"Bah!" grunted the humiliated mother. "I never want to set my eyes upon her face, be it fair or foul!"

"But, mother," reasoned her daughter, "it is better for us, surely, to try and make the best of it all now – for the sake of appearances, at all events."

Mrs. Jonathan leaned back in her easy chair with the air of one utterly disgusted with the whole thing. But she was a shrewd, worldly-wise woman, and now that the first heat of her displeasure was over, she began to see the wisdom of her daughter's words.

No good could possibly come of opposing this unfortunate alliance. Already Dewla bore, by right, the name of Smith. No power could divest her of it. There was nothing left for her but to bear the disappointment bravely, hiding the natural feelings of deep chagrin from the prying eyes of her acquaintances, whom she felt sure would be only too glad to glory over her humiliation.

No matter what pain it cost themselves as a family, they must, in public, make the best of it, and receive this unwelcome addition with open arms.

"You are a wise girl, Etta," she said at length, after a prolonged silence. "We must keep our feelings entirely to ourselves, and let none read the inner thoughts of our hearts. A family disturbance, such as this, should never be made known to the public; it is always a profound mistake. Your brother Hugh and his wife must come here, when the honeymoon is over, and we will introduce her, if she is at all presentable, to our friends."

"But, mother," broke in Mabel, "supposing, as is most probably the case, this girl is unrefined, uneducated, and vulgar. What then can we do? I should die with shame!" But as she spoke, the young woman looked all three herself.

"I am sure no nice-minded girl would rush into a marriage with a man whom she had only known a few days – the very idea is appalling." And Margaret tossed back her heavy, black fringe with an impatient gesture.

"Such marriages are not uncommon in Ireland, particularly in the Western districts," returned Mrs. Jonathan. "Not, indeed, that I have any desire to approve of the circumstances. On the contrary! I am more displeased than you can at all suppose, for I had widely-different views and plans for my only son, who might have married almost anyone. Indeed, I hardly know how I am to face Mrs. Sedley, after the suggestive hints I have dropped from time to time. How poor Hugh could have been persuaded into such a match is beyond my comprehension. He, of all others, so sober-minded and cautious."

"I wish he'd sent a photograph," said Etta musingly. "I do wonder what she's like, as regards looks. The Irish are said to be extremely handsome as a race."

"Pooh!" cried Mrs. Jonathan disdainfully. "Good looks are but poor substitutes for other things. But let us hope that she does possess even that one redeeming quality. As it is, I simply dread to think what she may be like!"

"It is the first romance we've ever had in our family," laughed Etta. "It seems too funny to believe quite."

Mrs. Jonathan frowned. "Do not speak so flippantly," she said severely. "If it is the first, as you remark, I sincerely trust it will also be the last."

And Etta, decidedly snubbed, said no more.

Mabel was pouting. "I think, on the advent of her coming, I shall take the opportunity to make it convenient to be away from home. I have a long-standing invitation to Scotland, as you know."

"I daresay we should all like to act thus, Mabel," returned her mother, "but such a course is out of the question. I am afraid we must consider your brother, and, for his sake, nerve ourselves for the ordeal. One thing more he must never guess how great a blow this unhappy news has been. Even if we do find his wife as objectionable as we fear, we must, nevertheless, hide from him our true feelings. It would only make a man, such as Hugh, cling to her all the more, and might cause a division between us forever. In his presence, at least, we must treat her with every outward appearance of respect."

"And when he is *not* there?" questioned Mabel.

Mrs. Jonathan did not answer. But her eyes narrowed, as if a new scheme had come to her mind.

CHAPTER VIII

"HUGH, have we much farther to travel? This seems a long train journey."

"Not so far now," was the cheery answer. "About an hour more, and we shall be safely landed at home."

At home! How strangely the words sounded in Dewla's ears, for the only home she had ever known lay far, far away, in a distant corner of Ireland.

It was nearly a month since she had taken a tearful farewell of the dear old place – dear, in her eyes still, though dilapidated and somewhat neglected. Her husband, seeing how much she loved it – though why she should puzzled him – decided not to sell the impoverished estates. The O'Donough had suggested to keep it just to please Dewla, with her old nurse installed as caretaker. For this act, Hugh earned his young wife's lasting gratitude. When she tried to express her thanks, words failed, and she only wept aloud.

Hugh was secretly touched by her love – nay, reverence – for the old place, not understanding how deeply attached the Irish are to the historic homes of their forefathers, be they ever so humble or poor.

After the first shock of her father's death had worn off, Hugh took Dewla away from Claisín. Since then, they had travelled about to many places, because Hugh hoped that the change of scenery would restore her usual brightness of spirits. Nor was he altogether disappointed. She gradually grew more cheerful and entered into his plans with more interest. Moreover, the roses were stealing back once more to her dimpled cheeks, and when she laughed, the sound had the old ring of mirth again.

"Do you think your mother will like me, Hugh?" Dewla looked up very wistfully into her husband's face.

"Why, of course, you foolish child. How could she help doing so?" Hugh smiled at her eagerness.

"I do hope she will," she continued in a low voice with its pretty, soft accent. "I have never known a mother's love, and it will be so sweet to feel that I have a real one now – and sisters, too. How rich you have made me, Hugh! And, too, just at a time when I was left so alone and friendless in the world. Except, of course, for the poor tenants and servants, I had no one else to turn to." As she spoke, her eyes shone with gratitude.

As the train sped on its way, the young man's thoughts grew a trifle uneasy. What if, after all, his mother did not approve of the step he had so suddenly taken? Her letters were just a little cool of late, he fancied. But no; perhaps it was only imagination on his part. In any case, to see and know his sweet little wife, would be to love her, too.

"How black the country looks, Hugh!" It was Dewla's voice which broke in upon his reverie.

"Yes; you see, we are getting into the pottery district now. It is all so smoky there. You will miss the proverbial green of your native isle, I fear."

"But don't you live in the country?"

"Why, no! We are located close to Hanley, and get a rather too-plentiful supply of soot and smoke."

"Oh!" was all Dewla said, but she looked disappointed. The prospect of living so far from the sweet, green grass of the country, such as she had been used to from babyhood, was not pleasant to contemplate.

"See, Hugh!" she cried suddenly, "how red the sky is! There is a great fire somewhere."

"Oh, no, that is the light from the furnaces. We shall see them presently as we pass."

"It does seem such a strange country," she went on, peering out through the closed window into the deepening twilight. "It makes me feel afraid, somehow."

"Foolish child," Hugh replied softly, putting his arm about her. "What makes you feel afraid?"

"I don't know," she almost sobbed, clinging to his hand. "I never felt like this before, and I ought not to, seeing that I am going to your home."

Gently he tried to soothe away her fears. "You will be all right in a little while," he whispered encouragingly. "I daresay the journey has been too much for you. I should have broken it halfway, only I thought it better to get home. Well, it is nearly over now. See! Those are the Etruria lights yonder. We shall be at our destination in less than no time, and then you shall have a long, long rest. So, cheer up, little wife."

Dewla smiled, though a cold, nameless dread of she knew not what had taken possession of her breast. Nor could she shake it off.

Only a little while more, and they steamed into the big station at Stoke, noisy and busy, as usual. Dewla, unaccustomed to so much bustle, was glad when she found herself safely installed in the waiting carriage sent by Mrs. Jonathan from Trafalgar House.

"I am sorry one of the girls did not turn out to meet us," Hugh said apologetically, as he took the vacant seat opposite. "Do you feel cold? Your hands trembles so."

But Dewla shook her head. She, too, wondered that none of her husband's family had come to bid her welcome, though she said not a word of this.

Through the crowded thoroughfares they drove. The shops on either side, gaily lighted, were a new sight to the country girl, and she watched the hurrying crowds of people with wondering eyes.

"What a big place this seems," she said, looking up into her husband's face. "I am afraid I should lose my way, were I to venture out alone!"

He laughed softly at her words. "Just wait till you've seen London," he answered. "I must take you for a run up to town as soon as I can manage it. You'd like it, would you not, Dewie?"

She hesitated a moment before making any reply, then, seeing that he expected her to speak, she said wistfully, "I am afraid you will think me very funny, but I think I should rather go somewhere into the country. London, like this, is full of people and noise. I do so love and prefer the quiet fields, and all the beautiful things of nature growing there."

Hugh laughed again. Then he said, somewhat quickly, "I am certain none of my people will agree with you in those tastes. Rural pursuits are not much in their line!"

The carriage presently turned into a by-way and drew up at a large house from which there seemed to flash a perfect glare of lights. A moment more, and Dewla found herself standing in a handsome hall. Here, her husband somewhat nervously presented her to a very stout lady, resplendent in sparkling diamonds and costly gown, behind whom clustered the three daughters of the house.

"Welcome, my dear." The great lady just touched the stranger's soft cheek with her purply lips.

The tone of her voice chilled the warmth of Dewla's young, tender heart. She instinctively felt no mother's love awaited her here. How different was this cold reception to what she had anticipated!

In vain she turned to the three new sisters-in-law, who each, in turn, pecked at her cheek with a murmur of greeting. She beheld no trace of affection on their stolid faces.

With an insuppressible shiver, she stood by with downcast heart, listening to her husband's voice as he stood a little aside, talking to his mother, answering her questions. Then, with one accord, they all filed into a large apartment to the right – a room which, even at this critical moment, caused Dewla to marvel at its magnificence and grandeur.

They had but barely crossed the threshold, when Mrs. Jonathan suddenly stopped. "My dear," she began blandly, addressing her daughter-in-law, "how remiss of me. Duncan," she added, in a louder voice to a waiting domestic, "show your mistress to her rooms. I hope," she continued, turning again to Dewla, "that you will not be too fatigued to dine with us, at eight."

"No, I thank you," murmured the girl, in a low voice. She longed intensely, all the while, that she might beg to be excused – only her courage failed before the frowning grandeur of Hugh's mother.

With a sigh of relief, she quitted the room and followed the maid's direction up the broad staircase made beautiful with statuary and palms. The powerful electric light, blazing on all sides, pained her tired eyes. She longed for the dulled luster of the old-fashioned lamps adorning the home of her childhood.

Very beautiful was the room into which she was ushered by the ceremonious handmaiden, her luggage having preceded them. Dewla longed to be left quite alone, but, evidently, this luxury was not for her. Already the domestic had unlocked the trunks, and was swiftly unpacking their contents.

"Dinner will be served in half-an-hour, madam. Please, which gown shall I lay out for your use?"

Dewla had not a large supply to choose from, and most of them were black, in consequence of her recent loss. Unaccustomed to the attentions of a lady's-maid, she very unwillingly accepted the proffered help, resigning herself into the skillful hands of the young waiting woman, who could not suppress an exclamation of surprise as Dewla's beautiful hair fell unbound to her knees in a shining cloud of golden brown.

With deft fingers, the rippling strands of hair were quickly coiled high upon the well-shaped head, much to the dresser's satisfaction, but Dewla herself was utterly indifferent just then as to how she looked – her heart felt sad and lonely. Mrs. Jonathan's cool reception had stung her proud, sensitive nature to the quick.

"They none of them want me!" she cried within herself. "I knew I would be miserable here. But it is Hugh's home. For my dear husband's sake, I must be patient, and try to win their love – if, indeed, they have any to give me!"

CHAPTER IX

"HUGH! Hugh! I wish you hadn't ever brought me here. I hate it all! Oh, how I hate it!" And the weeping girl hid her face on her folded arms, and sobbed aloud.

Dewla had only been at Trafalgar House a month, and yet it was growing almost unbearable – had been unbearable, indeed, from the very first – but lately things had gone worse. Her new relations took less care to hide their real feelings towards her, especially when Hugh was absent, as, of course, he usually was most of the day, being engaged at his office.

It was not often that the girl's proud spirit broke down thus, but today she was all alone in her room, with no fear of interruption, so she gave way to her long-pent-up tears, knowing that no one would see them.

It was a dark, gloomy day, late in December, cold and wild outside, and, despite the warm fire burning in the polished grate, Dewla shivered.

"I was never dull and miserable at home," she moaned, raising her wet eyes, and gazing out on the dismal housetops opposite. Oh! How wretched was the view! Not a tree or blade of grass to be seen – only the smoky chimneys and black, soot-grimed buildings.

"Outside and inside, it all feels the same – miserable! I must tell Hugh to take me away. I can't stay here, where no one cares for me. When he is not present, they laugh at my Irish ways and words, till I feel so, so wicked. Oh! I am ashamed of myself. What would dear father say if he knew?

"Hugh isn't quite the same as he used to be, either; I know it is his mother's doing. She does not like me one little bit. I can see it more plainly every day. She and her daughters are always hinting about people being *common*, and I know quite well they mean me!" And at this Dewla's eyes sparkled with anger, and the delicate color of her cheeks deepened to crimson.

Unable to control her indignation any longer, she paced up and down the room, her small hands clasped tightly together.

After a while, she grew calmer, and, taking the chair by the little table in the window, she sat down again, looking up at the dull, grey sky. How dark it appeared! Hugh had said that morning, that it looked like snow – and why, yes, it was beginning to fall. Just in tiny, stray flakes at first, then faster and thicker, until presently the dark masses of ugly, sooty stonework were transformed, as though by magic, to a sheet of pure, unsullied snow.

In delight, Dewla sat watching the beautiful change. How silently and quickly it had been wrought! No sound had been made by the feathery, white flakes floating softly to earth.

"Oh, it reminds me of my dear home!" she cried, a tender smile upon her lips. "I can almost see the old place once again. And how I loved to wake up in the morning, just to find hill and dale tree-top and pathway crowned alike with the fair, glittering snow!"

Musing thus, Dewla's heart was softened by memory's touch; the old, tender light beamed upon her face, chasing the dark cloud away. Suddenly, back to her mind came a verse, which had been one of her father's favorites.

"Wash me, and I shall be whiter than snow." Clasping her hands together, she sank upon her knees and prayed long and earnestly that the dark thoughts of her heart might be forgiven, and washed in the precious blood of the Lamb, who was slain that He might bear the sins of many.

In the twilight of the short December day she lingered thus, praying until a sweet sense of peace stole into her troubled breast, for she had come to the One great and true Friend, who was able and willing to comfort and help her in her loneliness.

Beside the richly-curtained window she crouched, her eyes feasting upon the white scene without. Oh! How fair it looked. Could it really be smoky, dingy Hanley? which never seemed like home to her!

Again her thoughts wandered off to distant Kerry. How lovely the great, silent woods must look just now, clothed, too, in this soft mantle of snow. She seemed almost to see, by fancy's magic power, the hoary branches of the spreading pines, weighed down with their burden of unmelted snowflakes.

How she used to love to wander out-of-doors and gaze about upon the new, white world, lovely in the sunshine, with the snow sparkling and flashing in the rosy light; yet more lovely still with the pale, solemn moonbeams stealing down upon it, with a weird and ghostly beauty all its own.

It seemed so strange to Dewla, accustomed all her life long to an outdoor life of perfect freedom, that now she must remain shut indoors, except for an occasional drive or short walk. Was it any wonder, then, that her spirit pined, like a caged bird's, for her old, unfettered life, unbound by custom or the dictates of a fashionable world?

Presently a step sounded upon the landing, and then the door of her room opened. It was Hugh, coming to seek his wife.

"What, Dewla! You here, and alone, in the dark? What a funny child you are." He came over to where she crouched beside the window, taking the vacant chair at her side.

"Oh! Hugh," she cried, lifting her beautiful eyes to his, her face all radiant. "I am so happy, watching the soft, drifting snow. It makes me think of – of home!"

Her low, sweet voice faltered a little as she uttered the last words.

The unconscious pathos of her words struck the young man keenly, and he drew the slight, childish form tenderly towards him, saying gently, "Are you not happy here, Dewie? Is not this your home, too?"

But she shook her head a little, not trusting herself to speak. It was not often that he spoke to her thus.

Hugh Smith mused within himself for a moment or two. Then he began quickly, as though with an effort. "I do not want to be harsh with you, dear. Heaven knows nothing is further from my thoughts – but is it not a little of your own fault that you are not more contented here? My mother and sisters do all in their power to make your life happy. What is wrong, Dewla?"

But again the girl was silent. Her nature was too sweet and loyal to wound him, by telling him the many ways in which his mother and sisters tried to irritate and wound her. She, of all others, would never set him against his own family. If she suffered, it must be in secret.

"Well!" he said, after a long silence, "if, as it seems, you have no grievances to relate, will you not make up your minds to be more agreeable, more pleasant in your manners? You sit so silent and quiet, that sometimes I fancy your thoughts are ten thousand miles away!"

A hot tear rolled slowly down Dewla's cheek, and fell, unnoticed, upon her hand.

"Will you not try and mix more with our friends? You will like them, and it will improve you, besides giving you more interest in your life. You will, to please me, put aside your mourning a little, and join us when we entertain. My mother wishes it, and so do I."

Dewla had bowed her head upon her clasped hands. She had felt each word he said – and she could read, beneath it all, Mrs. Jonathan's own ideas. It was she who had commissioned Hugh to take her to task thus.

Instantly her quick Irish nature rose up hotly in rebellion; then, as suddenly, the fire of her anger died away, for was not this woman her husband's mother? As such, she must respect her, and be silent.

In a voice strangely quiet, she said, "I am ready to do all that you wish, Hugh."

And he, delighted at the easy victory he had gained, kissed her brow, thoroughly satisfied with the result of his carefully-prepared lecture.

Hugh Smith, as before remarked, was a fair type of the ordinary English man; not remarkably handsome, perhaps, yet far from plain. He had a square-cut face with heavy brows, and a tawny, drooping moustache. His eyes were a deep blue grey, calm and earnest, always looking men fully in the face, having nothing to fear or conceal from any. He was a man singularly true and simple-minded; one who was honest, brave, and deeply sincere. A man, moreover, with nothing romantic or very interesting about him, and to whom life had always been more serious than idle. Naturally of a decidedly prosaic temperament, his life had hitherto been spent in calm, contemplative serenity — until his unexpected meeting with Dewla.

He little understood the true character of the shy, beautiful girl whom he had made his wife – beautiful in the highest sense of the word, not in person only, but in mind and heart. She had her faults, as who has not? But they were very lovable ones.

However, Mrs. Jonathan searched for these faults alone, and secretly magnified them in her son's unwilling eyes.

From the very beginning, she heartily disliked the proud, sensitive Irish girl, whom she was forced to receive as daughter-in-law. As the weeks went by, her dislike grew even greater, as the jealous mother saw that she was robbed of her son's first love.

Now his wife came first, usurping Mrs. Jonathan's place. Before herself, and all the world, Hugh thought only of Dewla.

Dewla was so unlike most girls – fearless and brave, yet gentle and sweet, disliking anything approaching flattery, utterly indifferent to admiration. She had lived so much alone all her life, thinking and studying deeply, that now, the constant talk and ceaseless chatter of strangers chafed upon her sensitive nature. She longed to run away, and leave them all far behind. "This strife of tongues," she called it to herself. But of all this she said naught to her husband. He was ignorant of the many petty, thinly-covered insults that were daily thrown at his young wife when he was not present.

As a result, from the beginning of her stay at Trafalgar House, Dewla had entreated to be excused from all society, pleading the fact of her recent bereavement. This Hugh had willingly granted, anxious to spare her all unnecessary pain.

But tonight, his mother had urged him into speaking on the subject to Dewla, declaring that people thought it most strange, not meeting his bride, or seeing her at any entertainment.

"Is he ashamed of her?" the public was beginning to ask.

Stung by this, he had made up his mind to talk it out with Dewla.

Besides, the old lady had hinted that such constant retirement was bad for the girl, as she was growing pale and morbid. Her son, thinking she spoke from kindly motives, thanked her gratefully for the mother-interest she evinced in his wife's welfare, saying he would see what his influence would do in the matter.

And thus it was he sought the fair recluse, believing that her continued moping was really injuring her health, and the cause of her pale cheeks and nervous manner.

"Dewla," Hugh went on, not seeing her face clearly in the deepening gloom; "tomorrow night, Mother will hold one of her weekly receptions. I want you to come down. You won't refuse me, will you?"

"No," Dewla answered again, in the same strained voice.

"And, if it is not asking too much, would you put aside your heavy black? Mother objects to it, on the ground that it looks out-of-place for a bride; but this I leave entirely with yourself, dear."

Dewla did not answer, but her head sank lower upon her breast. She was still deep in mourning for her dear father, but even this had to be cast aside for her mother-in-law's dictates.

It was another one of her petty cruelties – but Dewla would obey, though it cost her heart much to do so.

CHAPTER X

THE following night found Dewla obedient to her husband's wishes, to the very letter. Her mourning put entirely aside, she stood before the long mirror, arrayed in white. Not a single touch of black marred the soft, dazzling purity of her trailing robe.

Duncan fairly broke out into raptures over her young mistress, as she gave the last finishing touches to her toilet, declaring she had never seen anything more lovely.

Dewla turned away, for the sight of her lovely clothes pained her. This festive array seemed but a hideous mockery, because the heart that lay hidden beneath was sad and heavy.

"I wish it was all over," she cried, covering her face with her hands.

The maid looked up in surprise, but Dewla, unconscious that she had spoken her thoughts aloud, stood quite still, in the attitude of one who prays. Silently the wondering maid left her thus, stealing softly from the room.

It was Dewla Smith's first appearance in society. A low murmur greeted her as she entered the crowded drawing-room. Hugh himself was completely taken by surprise, for he had never seen her look more beautiful. Her cheeks, usually pale of late, were flushed, and her eyes flashed and sparkled with an unnatural luster.

Everyone was eagerly begging to be presented to the reigning beauty of the hour, who seemed so unconscious of the profound sensation her appearance was producing. She neither knew nor cared. It was Hugh's wish to have her present, not her own; but she meant to obey him in all things, both great and small, cost her what it might.

A tall, fair man, with a profusion of curly hair and deep-blue eyes, led her to a vacant seat, then stood next to her, talking to her in low, easy tones. Dewla had felt attracted to him from the first, simply because he reminded her of her cousin Charlie. He introduced himself as Mr. De Vere. They talked on many subjects. He was immensely interested as he listened to her unfavorable impression of the pottery districts, so fearlessly proclaimed, even though her sister-in-law quickly joined them, sitting within earshot. Etta was listening, too, smiling every time Mr. De Vere spoke, then switching to a disapproving glower when Dewla replied.

But when Dewla spoke of Kerry, her whole face changed, glowing with enthusiasm as she described the wild, beautiful scenery of wood and dale, forest and plain.

"I am half-Irish myself," smiled her companion, "though, indeed, I have never been to the Emerald Isle; that is a pleasure yet to come!"

"Oh, you are sure to like it," she returned eagerly. "The people are so nice. The peasantry, in particular, you will find witty and amusing. Of course, I allude now to Kerry, where my home has always been."

Mr. De Vere watched her expressive face with deep interest. There was something about her so fresh and bright, something which seemed to breathe of sweet heather and shamrocks green – a rare, pure waft of country breezes.

Music was the order of the evening; someone had volunteered to play a heavy, elaborate piece. This was followed by a song from one of the men.

"Will you not favor us with a little Irish ballad?" a lady enquired of Dewla when there was a pause.

Dewla looked up quickly to meet a pair of soft, grey eyes fixed upon her face in a friendly, scrutinizing manner. She had noticed this woman before, and liked her appearance.

"I sing so little," she faltered shyly, "and there are many here who can do so much better."

At this moment, Hugh was seen making his way to where they sat. Immediately Dewla's new acquaintance seized upon him.

"Mr. Smith," she cried eagerly, "I am trying to persuade your wife to sing. Do, please, add your vote also."

Hugh looked surprised. "Really, Mrs. Wardell," he replied, lifting his brows slightly. "I fear you are demanding an impossibility, for, as far as I know, Dewla is not musical."

"Oh, then you are extremely ignorant," retorted the other, "because she has already committed herself."

"Eh?" he said, his eyes resting admiringly upon his wife's beautiful face. "Is it so, Dewie?"

"I do sing just a little," she confessed. "If you desire to hear me, why, I will try to do my best."

"Bravo!" cried Mr. De Vere emphatically. "You see, we have won a victory, Mrs. Wardell."

And, without further ado, Dewla was borne off in triumph to the piano.

Playing her own accompaniment, she sang one of Moore's familiar Irish melodies in a sweet, true voice. Everyone listened as the rich notes rang out, clear as a bird's. When she had finished, her listeners applauded and asked for more.

Hugh was simply amazed; he could hardly believe his own ears.

Mrs. Jonathan was equally astonished, but her surprise was not as pleasant a one. She did not like all this fuss over Dewla, while her own daughters remained almost unnoticed. Secretly she wished that the girl had been allowed to have her own way, and abide longer in seclusion.

"It was foolish of me to press the point with Hugh," she grumbled to herself, with a sigh of disappointment.

Mrs. Wardell was a striking-looking woman, with eyes which could be soft and gentle, cold and harsh, just as the owner's mood chanced to be. From the first moment that she beheld Dewla, she took a strange fancy to the fair, young bride, and there and then made up her mind to be her friend.

From the little she knew of the great lady of Trafalgar House, and her three daughters, she wisely conjectured that the girl's sojourn here would hardly be an enviable time all round.

Later in the evening, she sought Dewla out again. "My dear," she began unceremoniously, "I have started making flannels for our brave, wounded soldiers who have been fighting so nobly at the front. Could you spare time to come to my house and help me a little?"

Dewla's face shone with sympathy. "Oh, I should just love it," she cried, with that characteristic warmth of manner peculiar to the Irish. "When may I come, please?"

Mrs. Wardell smiled. "Tomorrow, if you are not otherwise engaged."

Dewla shook her head. "I have no engagements," she answered quickly, "and I should like to help you so much, because I have a cousin out there." And her lips quivered a little, as she thought of bright, merry, light-hearted Charlie, who may, even now, be numbered among those wounded.

Hugh came up at this moment. "Well!" he said gaily, "what are you looking so serious about?" He touched his wife's arm gently.

"I am soliciting her services in my work, on behalf of the invalided soldiers," returned Mrs. Wardell, "and Mrs. Smith has most kindly responded. I will send the carriage round for her tomorrow, at three. Will that suit, please?"

"Beautifully!" cried Dewla, looking up gratefully into the kind eyes bent upon her.

"I did not know you were so deeply interested," said her husband, not a little surprised again.

"She has a cousin at the front," explained his mother, who had been a silent eavesdropper, "and, evidently, Dewla is *very* fond of him."

"Yes," replied her daughter-in-law unsuspiciously, "I am very fond of Charlie. He always lived with us, as long as I can remember."

"It is to him, evidently, you owe this depth of gratitude for Dewla's promised help," laughed Mrs. Jonathan.

Something in her voice sounded unpleasant to Dewla's ears, jarring harshly upon the momentary pleasure she felt at being able to add even her small mite of help in so good a cause.

"You must tell us more about this wonderful young man, my dear," continued Mrs. Jonathan in a smarmy voice. "Why have you been so reticent for so long?" She laughed again, but no one else joined.

Dewla felt the hot color rush to her face, but she stood silent. She knew that her mother-in-law was having some joke at her expense, though what it was she could not quite tell.

It was De Vere who came to the rescue, with timely tact.

"I really fancied, Mrs. Smith," he began quickly, "that the Irish were in favor of the Boers. I am glad to find even one noble exception, I assure you."

Dewla lifted her downcast eyes with that swift movement peculiar to her when amused.

"You mistake," she answered smiling. "We Irish are most loyal. Why, you must admit how splendidly the Irish regiments have acquitted themselves in this war. What would you have done without such men as Lord Roberts, Kitchener, Sir George White – who held Ladysmith for the Queen – and many others?"

How beautiful she looked at that moment, her eyes kindling with enthusiasm, and her cheeks flushed.

Hugh was watching her face closely; he had seldom seen her thus.

"It is easy to see that your *heart* is in the matter, my dear," assured Mrs. Jonathan, with unsubtle insinuation.

No one spoke for a second. Then Mrs. Wardell said to Dewla, in low, kindly tones:

"Irish girls are very clever at needlework, are they not? I have read so much about the beautiful handiwork executed by even the peasantry there."

"I am afraid I do not excel in that way," Dewla said with a smile. "I am ashamed to say I never took any trouble to learn to sew properly. I liked better to be out-of-doors all day long in sunshine or in snow – it mattered not, either was delightful."

"With your cousin Charlie, my dear?" broke in Mrs. Jonathan.

"Yes, of course, when he was at home, and not too busy with his books."

"We all enjoyed your sweet Irish song," said Mrs. Wardell, all but dragging her away from Mrs. Jonathan. "It was ever so pretty. Perhaps you will sing just one other?"

Dewla was looking at her husband's face. Had she somehow displeased him? Now he was watching her with smileless lips.

"What shall I sing, Hugh?" she enquired wistfully.

"Oh, anything you please," he retorted in an altered tone, turning away abruptly from the little group. The next moment he had taken a vacant chair beside a pretty, fair girl, whose blue eyes lit up when he started talking with her.

"Oh! I see Hugh has found Bella," crowed Mrs. Jonathan, following him with her eyes. "How *devoted* they used to be to each other."

Dewla's cheeks had suddenly paled. She stood quite still, her eyes riveted in the same direction.

"Are you not going to let us hear your voice again?" enquired Mrs. Wardell, anxious to divert the girl's attention. "See, Mr. De Vere is waiting to conduct you to the piano."

But Dewla shook her head. "I would prefer not to, if you do not mind," she answered slowly. All the flush and brightness had died out of her face, and her voice quivered as she spoke.

Mrs. Jonathan smiled in a very self-satisfied way.

CHAPTER XI

THE friendship between Mrs. Wardell and Dewla grew apace. Over the piles of flannel they talked, while their busy fingers nimbly stitched.

The cloud, small at first, which began to gather about Dewla's life at Trafalgar House, had grown darker and thicker now. Hugh had changed. Though kind and considerate for her comforts, as of old, he no longer flew to meet or seek her out upon his return from the office each day.

Vainly she pondered it all, with proud, hot tears shed in secret, but the only solution to the mystery seemed to be summed up in his mother's own insinuation that Bella Sedley the haughty, fair girl who had stared at Hugh so hard, had been more than a friend to him.

Dewla would often sit for long hours, thinking of this, making herself unutterably miserable.

"Now that he sees Bella once more," she moaned sadly, "he is sorry, for, of course, I am not beautiful as she is. Oh, Father, why did you compel us to marry? If only I could set him free once more! But that, alas, is impossible. No one likes me here. Mrs. Jonathan hates me. I feel, when I am with her, as though a cold, cold blast had swept about my heart, killing all its love and warmth. Oh! If only I could but run away anywhere far, far off!"

February had come in, bleak and cold changing to hard frost, so that rivers and brooks were ice-bound.

Mrs. Wardell remained Dewla's friend through these trying weeks, and often invited her to spend a long day with her, for which kindness Dewla was very grateful indeed.

One morning, when stormy March had dawned upon the earth, Etta was glancing carelessly over the war news of the day during breakfast-hour, reading out paragraphs of interest here and there.

"I say," she suddenly cried, addressing herself to Dewla, across the table, "isn't that cousin of yours in the Second Royal Irish Fusiliers? If so, they have had a hot time of it at Pieters Hill, preceding the relief of Ladysmith."

Dewla's face went white and scared. Her trembling lips refused to speak, hard though she tried to answer.

"Why, yes! Here's his name – dangerously wounded, too – Charles O'Donough Cooke."

A faint, suppressed moan, and Dewla's head sank backwards. For the second time in her life, she had lost consciousness. Once again, her husband's strong arms saved her from falling.

Tenderly he laid her upon the sofa, chafing the cold, listless hands in his.

"I didn't know she'd mind so much," cried Etta regretfully. "He was only a cousin, after all!"

Hugh winced at her words, but his mother laughed significantly. "Cousins are very *convenient* things," she said sharply, standing over Dewla, who lay unconscious upon the couch.

Then no one spoke for a while, each pondering Mrs. Jonathan's words. Hugh, who had been chafing her hands, slowed.

The color came slowly back to Dewla's cheeks. Soon she opened her eyes and sat up.

"Thank you," she said softly. "I don't know what happened…"

Hugh watched her coldly, waited until he was convinced of her recovery, then, bidding her rest for a while in grave, measured tones, he strode from the room and left the house, going to the office.

It seemed a long, long day to Dewla. Lonely and sad at heart, she sat by the fire in her own pretty room, choosing to remain there rather than encounter her mother-in-law, who ever looked upon her with cold, stern eyes.

Taking her Bible – the one which Dewla's mother had used and loved so well – she crouched upon the warm rug and opened the sacred volume, hoping for a message of comfort there. Nor was she disappointed. Almost the first words which met her gaze were these: "All things work together for good to them that love God." Her mother's hand had marked the verse with a pencil-line.

Evidently the sweet assurance that the great Ruler of all permitted and allowed the "all things" of life, declaring, in His infinite love and wisdom, that, though we cannot now understand the mystery, yet most surely are they working together for our eternal good.

Clasping her hands in prayer, Dewla bowed her head upon the open page, and pleaded for grace and help to leave everything, without reserve, in the Master's hand – her husband, first of all; then her poor, wounded cousin, so far away; and, lastly, herself and those with whom she dwelt, among whom her lot was cast.

With child-like trust and confidence, she brought each one by faith to the Savior's feet. As she prayed, the burden of her sorrow grew lighter, and the pain at her heart was stilled.

Before the dusk set in, there came a little note from Mrs. Wardell, begging Dewla to come and see her, as she wished to consult her on the subject of their work, over which they had so much mutual interest and sympathy.

Dewla would have much preferred to stay at home, for she felt so very sad, but did not like to refuse.

Consequently, in a short time, she came down, enveloped in cloak and hat, ready for her short walk.

Mrs. Jonathan regarded her daughter-in-law with consternation. "You cannot go alone," she said, in tones of authority.

"I am not the least bit nervous," Dewla replied quietly. "Please ask Hugh to call and fetch me home."

The great lady said no more, but her face wore a frown; she did not like being disobeyed.

Dewla found her new friend eagerly awaiting her arrival.

"It was so good of you to come," she began gratefully. "Take your hat off, please. Tom is out, so we shall have a long chat together, with no interruptions."

After the important subject of the work was settled, tea being over, Mrs. Wardell drew their chairs nearer the cheery fire, her quick eyes noticing a change in her young companion's face, particularly when in quiet repose. The eyes were more dreamy-looking, more tender and wistful in expression. Altogether, it was the face of one who suffered bravely, and in secret.

"Dewla," she began gently, after a lengthened pause, "you have told me the sad intelligence of your noble cousin's wounds. But, painful as I know by experience what such tidings are, still, may I ask if – if that is all that troubles you, dear child? For I can read you as one might read an open book, and I can see that your heart is troubled."

Dewla started, while the tell-tale color dyed her brow. The abruptness of the question threw her off her guard completely. Covering her face with her hands, she shrank back as though her friend had touched a sore wound.

In a moment, Mrs. Wardell was kneeling at her side.

"Dear child," she whispered softly, "tell me if you care to. I would help you if I could. You can tell me, surely?"

Dewla felt all her troubles crowding to her lips – all the grief that had filled her heart for all these months, ever since her father died. She so wanted to confess all to her friend.

But, by this time, Dewla's moment of weakness had passed and her usual self-control returned. She didn't want to burden her friend – or worse, drive her away – through a recital of her woes.

Lifting her head bravely, Dewla dashed aside the tears.

"I think the sudden news about my cousin has upset me, dear Mrs. Wardell," she said quickly. "Pray for my foolish behavior. I promise not to be such a … a little child again."

Only half-satisfied, the lady of the house rose from her knees. That Dewla had some hidden sorrow which she proudly locked within her own breast, she felt assured. Though she was disappointed that she was not allowed to share the secret, she honored and admired Dewla's loyal silence, wondering at the persistent self-control in one so young.

"These Irish are brave, true women," she thought, glancing with an admiration which bordered on reverence at the quiet, graceful figure opposite. "I wish I was not so fond of disclosing poor old Tom's small failings. If I were only more like her, we should both be happier."

Nothing more was said upon the subject, and Dewla made a strong effort to be as bright and cheerful as she could.

Thus the moments quickly flew, and it grew late. More than once Dewla glanced anxiously at the clock, wondering why Hugh did not come.

Presently a ring was heard. Feeling sure it was Hugh, his young wife rose from her chair with a sigh of relief.

But it did not happen to be Mr. Smith – only Duncan with the carriage. Her master had gone, with Etta, to spend the evening with the Sedleys, so Duncan been sent to fetch her mistress home.

Mrs. Wardell was quick to notice how Dewla's cheeks grew deadly white as she listened to the message. But no word fell from the girl's lips, though eyes were dark with sudden pain and disappointment.

Hugh had never treated her thus before, and her heart grew heavy with apprehension. In a quiet voice, though her lips were pale and smileless, she bade farewell to her hostess, and hurried away.

It was but a few minutes' drive to Trafalgar House, and yet, in that short space of time, how many swift, strange thoughts and fears passed through Dewla's fertile brain, all arising from the question, "Why had Hugh not come himself? Had something happened?"

Perhaps he loves me no longer, Dewla thought.

Did some shadow of the dark future fall upon her spirit then?

It did, for, despite the warmth of her rich cloak, black dread overtook her as the carriage drew up before the blazing, cold lights of Trafalgar House.

TO BE CONTINUED ...

"SWEET LITTLE SHAMROCK" is the title of our next story, Book 2 of the Shamrock Romances. It is an IRISH

Story, written by BIRDYE LATHAM HARTLAND in an unusually telling, helpful, and pathetic style, well-calculated to keep up the constant interest of every reader. Be sure to read it!

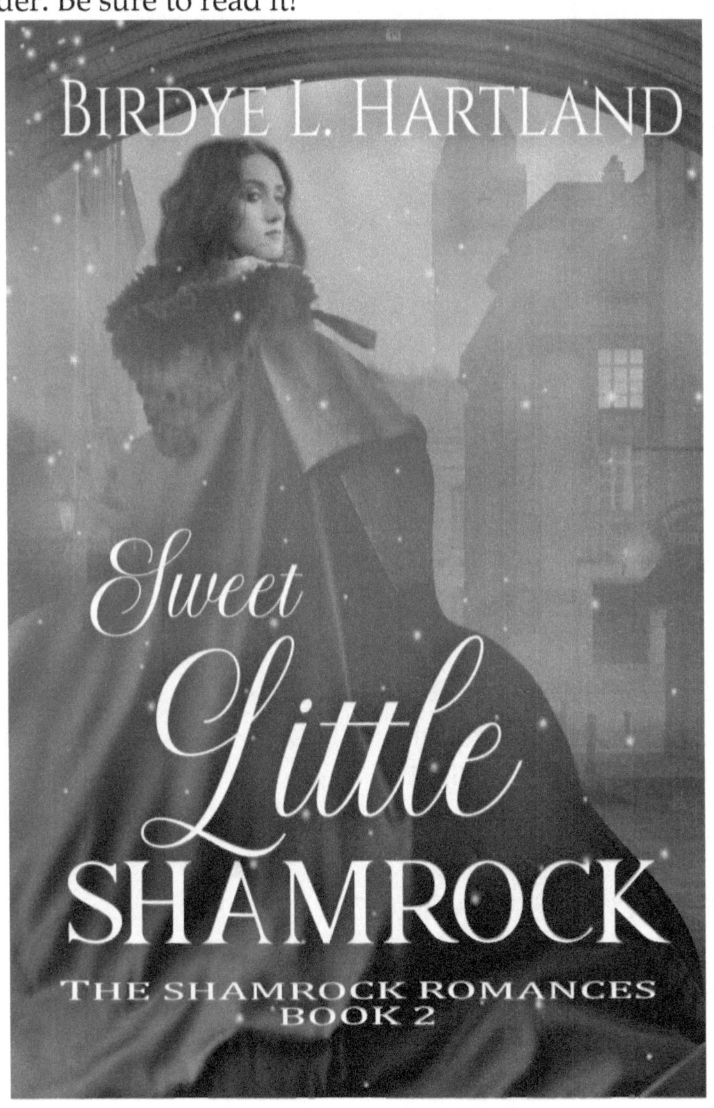

SWEET LITTLE SHAMROCK

A VINDICTIVE MOTHER-IN-LAW

Dewla Smith has never felt so alone. A newlywed far from her dear home in Ireland, her mother-in-law's petty cruelties only increase as Mrs. Jonathan chips away at her son's trust in Dewla. She is furious that this "wild Irish girl" is under her roof and is ready to do anything to ruin this marriage.

A TROUBLED MARRIAGE

Mrs. Jonathan's machinations are working, because Hugh is convinced that Dewla loves her cousin. Then when Hugh falls ill, Dewla stays at his sickbed, where they start to rebuild that fragile love … but some delirious words destroys that – and, to make matters worse, Mrs. Jonathan cheerfully invites Hugh's old flame to stay at their house and sit at his bedside!

WHAT IS WRONG WITH THIS WOMAN

After a terrible confrontation, Dewla, her heart absolutely broken, arrives on a final decision – a decision that sends her down a dark path, from which she might not return.

SWEET LITTLE SHAMROCK is the second book in the clean and sweet Victorian romance series, The Shamrock Romances.

This good old story from Victorian England has now been tidied up and shaken into shape by our chipper Victorian book fiend and tireless editor, Eva Valentine. You can find her on Twitter at @victorianreader and Tumblr at https://victorianworkhouse.tumblr.com/ posting from some lonely and wind-swept tower from the moors, where she's been locked by some cruel fiend. Oh, I hope she has an internet connection out there!

We here at Victorian Workhouse Press will be reprinting many more penny novels and old serials from those merry days of the 1890s. Stay tuned.

www.ingramcontent.com/pod-product-compliance
Lightning Source LLC
Chambersburg PA
CBHW021741190726
48288CB00009B/3122